The Snow Queen's Daughter

The Snow Queen's DAUGHTER

Serene Conneeley

Blessed Bee Books

"Kindness is like snow.
It beautifies everything it covers."

Kahlil Gibran, Lebanese-American poet

THE SNOW QUEEN'S DAUGHTER

Conneeley, Serene
The Snow Queen's Daughter by Serene Conneeley
ISBN: 978-0-6484016-4-3

Website: www.SereneConneeley.com
Email: blessedbeebooks@yahoo.com.au

Published by Blessed Bee Books
PO Box 449, Newtown, NSW 2042
Australia

Cover image: Olena Zaskochenko
Crown: Tatiana54
Snowflakes: Halina_Photo and Antuanetto

"Memory is the treasury
and guardian of all things."

Marcus Tullius Cicero, Roman philosopher

Chapter 1

Astrid couldn't remember a world without snow. Body aching and heart beating sluggishly in her chest, she stared out the window at the never-ending ice and frost that blanketed her existence. She couldn't recall what the ground looked like without its too-bright, glaring white coat, or imagine a sky in any colour other than dull, threatening grey.

Surely it had been different, once. As the tombstone chill of the ancient stone floor numbed her toes and snaked up her spine, wisps of memory tormented her, of thick emerald-green grass, sweetly scented rainbow-hued flowers, and sunrise skies in all shades of pink-lilac-gold. A tear trickled down her cheek, hot on her frozen skin, but she didn't even know why she was sad. It was a nameless dread, a sense of futility and mindless repetition. And a loneliness that crushed her soul.

Angrily brushing the teardrop away, she headed for bed. Still swathed in the many layers of thick clothing she'd been wearing all day, she burrowed down under the pile of heavy old quilts, praying the bone-deep cold would soon ease.

Crashing music dragged her back from a dream to her cold, bleak reality, and she groaned. She'd been walking along a golden beach, sun kissing her shoulders and gentle waves lapping at her feet, making her giggle when they danced up over her toes.

Now, her eyes misted, and she squeezed her lids shut. Couldn't she go back there? She'd been hand in hand with a boy, his grip tender yet firm, and he'd been smiling down at her, eyes sparkling with joy as he drew her close.

Joy at being with her.

She tried to picture the face of the kind stranger who had whispered that he loved her, but the threads of the vision floated away, dissolving like sea foam, while the sensation of his arms wrapped around her faded to nothing, leaving her shivering with cold once more.

The music picked up pace, and Astrid grudgingly gave up on sleep. It was the night of the winter solstice ball, and she knew the grand room downstairs would be filled with well-dressed sycophants making sure it looked like they were having a good time.

Sighing, she pulled a quilt around her shoulders and crept out of her bedchamber, tiptoeing along the empty corridor to the top of the ornate marble staircase that curved down into the ballroom. Nervously she peered over the edge of the banister, but she needn't have worried. No one was looking in her direction.

All eyes were on the imposing woman standing on the dais at the other end of the room. Draped in white furs, her blood-red lips and black-as-night hair were a chilling contrast to her icy blue eyes. Even from this distance, Astrid trembled at the remote and frosty expression covering the woman's face like a mask. She knew everyone in the crowd below was terrified of her, but there was no way they would stay away. No way they could. Queen Margrete demanded fierce loyalty from her subjects, and their attendance when she called for it was not optional.

Even though these formal occasions seemed to happen with alarming, confusing regularity. Astrid could have sworn the same ball had been held only a week ago, not a year. And the week before that as well.

But that made no sense. Desperately she tried to remember the last time she'd crouched up here in the darkness, watching the kaleidoscope of wintry dancers shifting below her. Tendrils of smoky half-memories drifted tantalisingly close, then glided out of reach. Shadowy glimpses of graceful gossamer-gowned women and mysterious velvet-clad men haunted her, insubstantial as ghosts. Or dreams.

Was she dreaming now? Stuck in a nightmare of an eternal winter? A shudder rocked through her. Sometimes it felt as though years had passed since she'd seen a blue sky. Her eyes darted to the huge ornate clock above the dais. Eleven pm, December 23.

The rose-gold clock face was illuminated by the stars on the minute and second hands, which chased the moon on the hour hand in an eternal dance. Below them, small copper figures stood poised, ready to flip over the cards that showed the day and month of the year.

The lavish feast had been eaten, and now the musicians were tuning up for a final round of dancing. But first, the Queen rose to her feet to address the crowd.

"Thank you, beloved friends, for being here tonight for our special Yule ball." Her voice boomed out, effortlessly filling the cavernous room, and the guests all gazed up at her, heads swivelling as one to offer her their full and complete attention. As though she was the sun they all longed for, the source of their warmth, rather than the woman of ice and frost that she actually was.

"May this magical solstice evening bring you joy and renewal, and hope in the darkness," she thundered. "This celestial point marks the moment that the sun begins its return, promising us all the gladness of springtime ahead. So let us dance in celebration!"

Astrid watched as the people below applauded wildly, curtseyed or bowed, then paired off and began to move in time with the now-jaunty music. They were like butterflies, their jewel-bright dresses or velvet capes fluttering as they linked hands then moved backwards, came together then spun apart, swirling around the room in a hypnotic, richly hued rhythm that defied the whiteness of the world they were trapped in. And while they continued their strange symphony, bodies ebbing and flowing like the tide, the Queen sat on her throne, cold and remote.

Finally someone had drunk enough mulled wine to be brave enough to invite her to join them, and the monarch allowed herself to be twirled amongst her subjects to the jubilant melodies of the orchestra.

Mesmerised by the spinning of the dancers, Astrid's eyelids started to flutter closed, and the visions that had been hovering at the edge of her awareness crowded in on her – two sisters, one black-haired, one blonde; a battle, a quest; a man blasted with ice. Then the high brassy notes of a trumpet pulled her abruptly back from the brink of sleep.

She blinked rapidly, trying to clear the fog from her mind, and the questions boring into her brain.

Crawling forward, she peered between the carved wooden balustrades. Five minutes to midnight. Time for the last dance. Astrid watched Queen Margrete gracefully remount the dais and recline on her throne, gazing out over the ocean of colour and warmth with narrowed, glittering eyes and a tight smile.

Slowly the second hand ticked its way around the clock's gilt-edged face, Astrid's heart hammering in time with it. Trepidation washed over her, but she tried to shake it off. She was being foolish. Fanciful. Time couldn't get stuck, or loop back on itself. Winter solstice was about to be over. In a moment Christmas Eve would dawn, time would move forward, and Christmas Day would roll around again, solitary and miserable as usual, no doubt, but then Astrid could start counting down to her New Year's Eve birthday. She would finally turn eighteen, and she could leave this wretched kingdom forever. She grinned in anticipation. Freedom beckoned. She could taste it.

The first chime of midnight struck, then the second, and Astrid held her breath, unable to arrest the anxiety thundering through her body.

The Queen rose, inclining her head regally to the crowd as another two chimes pounded out.

"Thank you for being here this evening!"

Another chime boomed out across the room.

And another.

"It has been wonderful to see you all."

Boom.

Boom.

Boom.

"Safe travels as you return to your homes to sleep sweetly and dream."

Boom.

Boom.

"And I hope you will all return next Friday night for our winter solstice ball!"

As she spoke the last word, the final stroke of midnight rang out, and the clock turned over. It was December 17.

Again.

Astrid slumped to the floor. The thick swirl of deja vu pressed down on her, crushing her body and her spirit. She didn't know how, or why, but it seemed that time really was reversing, repeating.

Trying to think straight through the brain fog and confusion pulling her under, she gazed again at the Queen on the dais. She couldn't remember the specifics, couldn't even hold on to a thought before it slipped away like the worst kind of traitor, but some part of her knew with absolute certainty that she'd sat up here before and watched this ball unfold. Had seen the date reset itself from the 23rd to the 17th on other occasions. She *was* caught in an endless time loop that made her want to scream.

When her mother glared up at her from the distant throne, she realised that this time she actually had.

Chapter 2

A gentle hand clutched Astrid's elbow, and her maid Kristina lifted her to her feet and hurried her back along the freezing stone hallway.

"Come on my lady, time for bed. It will be warmer in your chamber."

Astrid smiled absently, then looked more closely at the girl. Her cheeks were red with cold, and her lips were blue. For the first time, Astrid noticed she was shivering.

"Where's your coat? You'll freeze in that cotton shift."

Her companion stared at her, a frown marring her brow. "I don't have one my lady, this is what I always wear," she said stiffly.

"But it's so cold!"

"Gee, I had no idea," Kristina muttered under her breath. She urged her charge onwards, increasing their pace, before pushing her into her chamber and heaving the heavy door closed. "The Queen heard you scream, and she didn't look happy," she said, panic making her voice rise. "Quickly, into your nightgown and into bed. If the light is extinguished before she reaches this corridor, she may leave the reprimanding until tomorrow. We've got a head start, because she'll have to farewell her guests."

Astrid nodded, distracted. Did her maid know something strange was happening too, or was she just scared the monarch would blame her for Astrid's outburst? She allowed the girl to unhook the laces of her woollen dress and peel off the many layers of underskirts, then slip her nightgown over her head.

When her shoes were unlaced and her bare feet touched the cold stone floor, Astrid winced. Scrambling under the covers, she pulled them up to her chin, her teeth chattering and her whole body shivering. Her maid turned to leave, but Astrid clutched at her hand.

"Stay." Her words came out harsher and more demanding than she'd intended.

The girl stared at her, shocked, then quickly shook her head. "I can't."

She couldn't blame her. It wasn't like they were friends, or that she'd ever asked for her company before. Often days went by without her even speaking to her maid, let alone acknowledging her presence or thanking her for all she did for her. Had she ever thanked her? Asked how she was?

A pang of shame pierced Astrid's heart. She wasn't surprised the girl would rather be away from her, but she was so deeply unsettled by the echo of her scream and the image of the clock flipping back a week, that the thought of being alone in the dark in this draughty old castle was too awful to contemplate.

"Please," she begged, trying to make her voice kinder. "It's so cold out there. And…" She stopped, unwilling to reveal just how badly she ached from loneliness. How desperate she was for someone to listen to her, to hear her. To *see* her. A tear welled in the corner of her eye as she waited, terrified she would be rejected again.

Uncertainty warred with a longing for warmth in her maid's eyes, and for a moment Astrid expected her to refuse once more. But when they heard the heavy wooden door at the end of the corridor crash open against the stone wall, panic flitted across Kristina's face and she quickly nodded, slipping off her wooden clogs and blowing out the candle, then climbing demurely into the huge bed. Laying rigid on the very edge, she radiated discomfort, but couldn't stop the small sigh of pleasure escaping her trembling lips.

It was awkward, Astrid conceded, and she could sense the girl's unease. Had she crossed a line by inviting her to stay? Would it impact on their relationship going forward?

Not that they had much of a relationship. The Queen was very clear about the lowly status of all their servants, enforcing harsh punishments on any that didn't pay the proper deference to her, and encouraging her daughter to be equally dismissive. Astrid had seen the way they gazed after the monarch, resentment blazing in their eyes as they curtseyed stiffly in her wake. She was aloof and unbending, and suddenly Astrid wondered whether they saw her as a carbon copy of her mother. Uncaring. Unpleasant. Unkind.

Was she?

She rubbed her eyes. She had to focus.

Mind racing, she pushed aside her worries over how she was seen, and tried to order her thoughts. Tried to make sense of the ball and the dancers and that broken clock.

"Is something strange going on?" Astrid finally blurted out into the darkness. "Because it feels like this Yule ball has been held before, doesn't it? At least a few times now. Maybe every week?"

She barked out a harsh chuckle. It sounded stupid, now that she'd said it out loud. Not that it had sounded much more coherent in her head. "It feels like we're stuck in a time loop, in an eternal winter," she whispered, then paused, trying to muffle her laughter, which definitely had a hysterical edge to it. "Or is all of this just a nightmare I'm trapped in? That we're *all* trapped in?"

She waited for her maid to respond, but there was only silence, and she blushed. "No, wait. Don't worry. I'm just so cold and miserable, so depressed from this never-ending snow, that my brain is playing tricks on me, right?"

Astrid paused. Squirmed a little. Rolled her eyes at herself. That actually made the most sense, and a rush of relief softened her panic. How embarrassing though, that she'd said out loud that she believed in time loops and curses. "Never mind, I'm just being silly. Maybe I'm coming down with something. Sleep well Kristina."

Her maid moved restlessly beside her, as though summoning the courage to speak, but she only sighed. Astrid was on the verge of slumber when the other girl finally spoke, voice low and tentative.

"Cook was complaining about the bone-deep cold this morning. She said the storerooms are almost empty and we're nearly out of food, and although she's placed orders repeatedly, none have arrived. She warned us that if this snow keeps falling much longer, we'll all starve."

She trailed off, hesitating for a long moment, then lowered her voice even further. "She said it's never been like this before, not since before you were born, and that something must be... wrong."

The hairs on Astrid's arms stood up, and she shivered and edged a little closer to Kristina, desperate to feel her body heat, and to not feel so alone. Although she'd thought she wanted confirmation that something was wrong, hearing that others were worried too terrified her. Clearly all she'd actually wanted was reassurance that everything was fine. *Normal.* That she would wake up in the morning and it would be Christmas Eve, and the days would slowly start to lengthen as the sun moved back towards them and their icy kingdom, offering warmth and light and comfort.

"Are you all right, my lady?"

Sighing deeply, Astrid forced herself to relax, to seem unconcerned. "I don't know. I feel like I've been asleep for a long time, yet I'm exhausted. And my brain is fuzzy. Confused…"

Suddenly a memory struck her, from earlier that day. How on earth had she forgotten it? "I found a book of the most marvellous faery tales under my bed this morning. There's a story about a prince who rescues a princess trapped in a tower, and another about a princess who saves her sister from an evil sorcerer. But the strangest and most wonderful thing is that there's an inscription in it."

She paused, trying to grasp hold of the tendrils of recollection. "It was in an unfamiliar hand, and it said something like: 'Dear Astrid, I hope you love these stories as much as I do. It's been so wonderful spending time with you in the castle, like being in a real-life faery tale, and I can't wait to return. With love, Emilja.'

"Who on earth is Emilja?" she demanded, her loneliness exacerbated by the hint that she'd once had a companion. The promise that she hadn't always been lonely. Hadn't always been alone. "Surely I'd remember if I had a friend?

Someone who gave me presents? Someone who stayed the night with me here – a real guest?"

The full moon shone through the frozen window panes, and the scent of pine trees wafted through a crack in the frame where a draught snuck in. *Christmas trees.* "And Christmas," she whispered. The tear rolled down her cheek and onto her pillow. "It feels like it should be Christmas soon, but it never comes. That's crazy though, right?"

She felt Kristina stiffen beside her, then tremble, yet when she finally spoke her voice was firm. "Right. What you're saying is impossible. It's just been such a hard winter that it's making us all feel like it will never end. But it will. Get some sleep, my lady, you're just over-tired. I'm sure everything will be all right in the morning."

Astrid nodded. Could it be that simple? She did feel a little feverish, and an overwhelming weariness was trying to pull her back down into sleep. She wanted to surrender to it – yet Cook was worried too. And the Queen's eyes as she'd stared at her from the dais had been filled with warning, and something else...

Fear?

Something was going on, she was sure of it, but what was it? Why couldn't she remember? And what was her mother doing?

Chapter 3

A howling, restless wind woke Astrid, and she knew before she opened her eyes that she was alone in her freezing chamber. Her fingers reached out, seeking warmth. Had her maid stayed the night with her, sharing her fears in the darkness, or had she just imagined that?

Then she froze. And muttered a desperate prayer.

Please god, no!

She hadn't really screamed at midnight, in front of a ballroom full of guests, had she? Hadn't completely freaked out as she watched the huge clock tick over, then tick back a week, earning her mother's chilling wrath? Astrid's gut clenched in fear, and she wished she could hide under the covers forever. But there was no way she could avoid her fate.

Reluctantly she dragged herself out of bed, the ice-cold floor and freezing chamber sending shivers through her physical body, while the nameless dread crept along her spine and threatened to choke her. Struggling into a dress as glum as the drab grey sky outside, she forced herself down the stairs to breakfast, despair shrouding her like a cloak.

Her mother sat at one end of the long, narrow table, scooping out pomegranate seeds with a tiny gold spoon, and swallowing them between sips of thick dark coffee.

She glanced up with her usual icy expression. "Good morning, Daughter."

"Hello Mother."

Astrid took a seat, and smiled in gratitude as Kristina brought her a bowl of warm porridge sprinkled with brown sugar and lashings of melted butter. Dipping a curtsey, the maid returned to the kitchen with barely a glance at her, and Astrid decided she must have imagined their late-night conversation about an eternal winter.

Staring warily at her mother, she hoped she'd imagined her midnight scream as well.

"Have some coffee," the Queen commanded, pouring her a mug and pushing it along the table. "I can't believe we ran out for a week."

Shrugging, Astrid picked up the mug and took a long sip. The warmth was soothing, and the creamy taste and mellow aroma of the beans comforted her. She stared into the dark surface of the brew while her hands clung to the hot cup.

"Why are you moping?"

Jolting in her seat, Astrid's gaze darted back up. "I'm not moping," she began, but her mother cut her off.

"I won't have you upsetting my guests with your piercing, uncouth screams."

Astrid gasped. *No, no, no!* Her skin crawled with horror. She hadn't imagined it. Not that she'd screamed, or that a ballroom full of people had stared up at her, or that her mother had glared at her with malevolent rage.

Did that mean Kristina *had* stayed the night with her, and they really had confided in each other about their fears of eternal winter in the bone-chilling dark? But if that was true, why had she snuck out before Astrid woke? Why did she refuse to make eye contact with her this morning?

That was the least of her worries right now though. "Shouldn't a loving mother wonder why her daughter was screaming, not castigate her for it?" she asked, voice shaking far more than she'd like.

"Fine." The Queen put down her spoon, impatience etched into the deep lines around her mouth. "What is upsetting you, Daughter dear?"

Where did she even start?

"I'm just so lonely," Astrid finally whispered, surprising herself with the admission.

And scared, but she wasn't going to reveal that little secret to anyone.

"The castle is filled with people, and you see your tutors every day." Her cold-as-ice mother gazed at the mirror on the wall and smoothed her hair, having already dismissed her daughter's concerns.

"You're not even here half the week."

Her mother sighed dramatically and glared back at Astrid. "You know I have work to do. I can't be here every moment just to entertain you."

"I have no friends," Astrid moaned. Then she hid her pout, took a deep breath, and forced herself to speak calmly. "But I used to, didn't I? I had a friend called Emilja. What happened to her?" Tears welled in her eyes, but she willed them not to fall. Her mother hated weakness, so she would not give her the satisfaction of seeing her diminished to a blubbering mess.

Red blotches appeared on the Queen's cheeks, and her eyes narrowed. "How do you remember that?" she snapped, then cringed at what she'd admitted.

Wide-eyed with shock, Astrid stared at her. There was something she'd forgotten, something the book had unlocked. Her mind churned with this new information.

But her mother recovered her temper quickly, her face a study of control. "Fine. Yes, you did have a friend called Emilja, but one day you got angry at her, and lashed out, and she collapsed under the weight of your ice-fuelled fury. I had to pay her mother a lot of money, first for medical treatment, and then to silence her. The girl survived though, so I don't know what her problem was. But I digress."

Astrid froze in horror as a flash of memory burned itself into her brain, unfolding like a movie. She and a girl with long red hair were walking up the front steps of school together, laughing and chattering... *Friends.* Until the boy Astrid liked approached them, handed Emilja a pink rose, and invited her to the upcoming dance.

Her stomach twisted as she saw herself pushing the red-haired girl away, then grabbing the boy and shouting: "He's mine!" Recalled the rage sweeping through her body, blinding her, shutting her down, so she wasn't even aware of the storm clouds forming overhead that blocked out the blue sky, or the snowflakes that swirled around her in a wild, out-of-control blizzard – or the spears of ice that were flying towards her friend, dagger-sharp and directed by Astrid's own hands, heading straight at Emilja's heart.

Snow had blanketed the girl's clothes as she sank to the ground, her face a mask of pain and terror. Her long red hair was turning white, but it was her gasp of betrayal that finally brought Astrid back to herself. Somehow realising what she'd done, although she couldn't comprehend it, Astrid turned to flee. Only to see her mother gliding up the school steps, her voice soothing, her presence calming, her muttered words a spell to make them forget what her daughter had done.

A spell.

"You enspelled me too!" Astrid croaked, face pale and knuckles white as she gripped the edge of the table. Her revulsion was for her own actions though, not her mother's. How could she have hurt her friend, hurt anyone?

The Queen shrugged. "It seemed the right thing to do."

"But I'm a monster! I shouldn't have been allowed to forget that." Her mother's dismissiveness and lazy indifference were almost as horrifying to Astrid as what she'd done to Emilja.

"Oh, calm down. The people in the village are beneath you. The girl is fine. No one remembers. Drink your coffee."

Distracted, Astrid picked up her mug and took a sip, trying to find comfort in the warmth of the brew. Her thoughts whirred, image after horrifying image of what she'd done to Emilja tormenting her, but she swallowed the drink and did her best to pull herself together. "Is that why no one ever visits me? Why you forbid me from going to the village?" Her voice cracked, echoing the shattering of her heart. "Are they worried I'll hurt someone else?"

Her mother laughed callously. "Don't flatter yourself. They don't remember you."

"Oh." Crumbling in on herself, Astrid finally allowed her tears to fall. She wanted to plunge outside into the icy wasteland and expose herself to the elements. To let the snow freeze her blackened heart, and put an end to her. She didn't deserve friends. She didn't deserve to live. For a moment she thought of the soothing presence of her maid the night before, when they'd huddled together in the cocoon of quilts, talking. *Almost like friends.* But she couldn't be trusted to have one of those.

Is that why Kristina had snuck out before Astrid woke, why she could barely look at her now? Was everyone terrified of her, the same way they were terrified of the Queen? Her heart recoiled from the possibility.

Her mother drew herself up to her full height, shoulders squared, and glared down her nose at her daughter. "Oh for heaven's sake, stop your blubbering. You can come to the ball on Friday night, and I'll send an invitation to all the villagers who are your age. They'll be honoured and excited to be invited, and will understand how lucky they'd be if you deigned to talk to them. So you can have some little friends, if that's what you want."

She sniffed haughtily, as though she found the very idea repulsive. "Now go and order a new dress from my wardrobe mistress. I can't have you embarrassing me. And ensure that it's red and green, for the winter solstice."

A tight band of fear squeezed around Astrid's heart. *The constantly repeating winter solstice.*

Glaring at her daughter, Queen Margrete took a last sip of coffee then sighed impatiently. "Are you happy now? My work is waiting, I have to go. *Surely* you can manage for a few days, surrounded by your tutors and all our servants. You're not a child Astrid, are you?"

And she swept out of the dining room without waiting for a reply, her breath fogging in the chill that always swirled around her. Astrid listened as her mother fired off a stream of orders to the staff, voice harsh and imperious, then slammed the front door behind her. She had no idea where her mother was going, or even what she would be doing. Unleashing her icy magic on a country like Australia, to put out some bushfires? Or was it more likely that she'd create drenching rains in a land already flooding, or torment a mountain climber with fresh snow dumps and avalanches?

Surely not.

Her head spun. Was she imagining these scenarios because she was suddenly aware of her own destructive powers? Or had she somehow always known that her mother was dangerous?

Was she dangerous too?

The door opened quietly, and a tentative voice asked if she could enter.

Astrid frowned. "Of course."

"I'm sorry to interrupt you, my lady, but the Queen instructed me to start on your ballgown right away. When would be convenient for you to have a fitting?"

Pushing back from the table, Astrid stood up and forced a smile. "Erika, is that right?"

The woman nodded shyly, and dropped a curtsey.

"There's no need for that. And I can start whenever is convenient for you."

Still horrified by what she'd apparently done, she meekly followed the seamstress to a dress salon on the second floor, the first she'd ever heard of such a place. *Or was it?*

It was when they were walking along an unfamiliar corridor that Astrid stopped suddenly, hands flying to her mouth in shock. A huge painting was hanging on the wall, a painting she'd never seen before. A painting she couldn't make sense of.

It was of her and her mother, sitting together on a purple velvet couch, heads bent close as though they were in private conversation. Sunlight streamed in a window to the side, bathing them both in a golden glow, and they were beaming at each other, the love in her mother's eyes crystal clear.

Who had painted it? When?

She stared at the clothes of their painted selves, trying to remember when she'd ever worn such a joyful yellow confection, or her mother the frothy pink gown she was draped in. Peering closer, she guessed she must have been around twelve, so it was five or six year ago – but her mother looked decades younger than she did now. Her eyes were less narrowed, with none of their current bitterness, her lips less pinched, less harsh. Her whole demeanour was softer. *Loving.*

Walking a few steps further, Astrid gazed at another painting of mother and child, the two of them holding hands this time as they stood on the steps of the castle, a blue sky in the background, and a spray of pink roses twining around the entrance columns. It was maybe a year or two after the first artwork, but their happiness in each other's company was the same.

Likewise the next one, where it seemed the Queen was laughing, head thrown back in delight, at something her daughter had said. Astrid had never seen her mother laugh like that, had she?

"My lady?" Erika asked nervously, and Astrid realised she must have asked that question out loud. Flustered, she whispered an apology and followed her into the salon.

In a daze, she allowed herself to be weighed and measured, poked and prodded. To have swathes of luxurious fabric held up to her face in order to choose the most appropriate shade for her complexion, whatever that meant. To stand still for two hours while a team of people discussed her and her body as though she wasn't there. It was strange and exhausting, but she wasn't going to complain. She would never complain again.

Had these women sewn the dresses she was wearing in those paintings? Had they known her mother back when she was the smiling young queen portrayed on those walls?

If they had, they'd forgotten her. It was unsettling to realise how scared they all were of her mother, and the terror seemed to extend to her – they were nervous around her, and embarrassingly deferential, even though she'd never spent any time with them.

Or had she?

She tried to engage with them, asking them questions in the hope of sparking memories, but she saw fear in their eyes, heard it in their trembling whispers and sensed it in their reverent, overly polite gestures. The gulf between them was dismally clear. Had she been so self-involved that she'd never realised how they felt about working in the castle? How they were treated? How scared of her they seemed? She'd been so caught up in her own fear of her mother, and her awful feelings of inadequacy, that she hadn't spared anyone else a thought.

Some queen she would make when the time came...

She vowed to be better. To pay attention to those around her, and try to look outside of herself. And to quit moping. She laughed as she remembered her mother accusing her of moping that very morning.

It took the wardrobe mistress and her team most of the week to get the gown finished, and there were several awkward fittings, but when Astrid stepped into it for the final time on Friday afternoon, she gasped in astonishment at the transformation they had wrought, and noticed the deep satisfaction on Erika's face.

"Thank you so much, I love it," Astrid said, swirling around as she gazed into the mirror at her reflection. She looked almost pretty. Almost regal even.

And almost happy.

Chapter 4

Butterflies swooped around Astrid's stomach as she stood at the top of the stairs, gazing down into the ballroom. Last Friday night, and for who knew how long before that, she'd been a voyeur, hidden away upstairs as she watched everyone else have fun. Tonight, at last, she would be part of it all. And maybe tonight, the clock would tick over, and Christmas would finally arrive.

Descending the marble staircase, she marvelled at the beauty of the space below her. The far wall was all glass, the curtains pulled back to reveal the waning moon shining on blankets of snow. Strings of faery lights twinkled across the vast ceiling like fireflies, and the huge pine trees in each corner created a festive atmosphere, and added a warm fragrance to the air. Candles scented with cinnamon, nutmeg and other exotic spices burned in huge sconces, emitting an enchanting golden glow, and waiters moved gracefully around the edges with trays filled with chalices of ruby-red mulled wine.

Heart pounding, Astrid peered into the crowd, recognising a few of the satin-clad dancers from the previous ball. Each glanced at her in admiration, inclining their heads in greeting, and Astrid smiled as regally as she could in response. That afternoon her mother had instructed her on the haughty attitude she was to greet their subjects with, but she couldn't bring herself to do it. She was no better than these people, and didn't deserve to be held above them. Especially now she knew what she'd done to her friend.

Blushing with shame, she pondered fleeing, until she spotted a group of young, neatly dressed strangers hovering near the door, gazing around in awe and looking just as uncomfortable as her. Were they the villagers she'd been to school with, back before she'd known – then forgotten – that she had a dangerous power lurking within her, ready to explode outwards at any moment?

A vision paralysed her. A school playground, green grass, blue skies, and golden sunshine. Her legs buckled. There *had* been a time before this eternal winter.

Grasping the banister to stay upright, she stared down at her feet in their delicate, unfamiliar high heels, concentrating on the step below her. When she sensed the eyes of the villagers alight on her, she glanced up sharply, and they all froze. Now their awe was mixed with fear, but before she could wonder why, the castle steward hurried forward, bowed to her, and gently took her arm.

"My lady," he said softly, deferentially. "All of the young folk from the village are over this way, excitedly waiting to meet you."

He smiled at her, something like pride in his eyes. "And may I add, you look incredibly beautiful tonight."

Inhaling sharply as she tried to get her nerves under control, she nodded her thanks for the compliment, then glanced back the way she'd come. She longed to race back up the stairs and hide in her bedchamber, but this was what she wanted, right? To break out of her isolation and be among people. To have friends. To banish the loneliness she was drowning in.

But could these people ever be her friends? They lived just down the hill, yet it was a whole other existence. They never interacted. What must they think of her, hidden up here all alone, cut off from their world? Or had her mother spoken truth when she said they'd forgotten all about her?

She was about to find out.

One of the group saw her approaching, and his jaw dropped. He nudged the guy next to him, who spun around and looked her up and down, one eyebrow raised in... what was that expression?

All of a sudden the dress she'd loved so much that afternoon felt ridiculous, like she was playing dress-up in her mother's clothes. The fabric was stifling her, the too-tight laces made it hard to breathe, and she was terrified she would trip over and fall flat on her face as soon as she took another step.

"My lady –" the steward began, but she cut him off.

"Just Astrid," she said hastily.

He frowned, but led her over to the group with a resigned sigh. "Astrid, these are all the seventeen and eighteen-year-olds from the village down the mountain. Jonas here will introduce you to everyone, and I've set up the Blue Room in case you want to move somewhere quieter to talk. But you and your friends are welcome to stay here in the ballroom, of course." And he left her alone in the circle of thirteen teenagers. Thirteen teenagers who were all staring at her, shell-shocked and silent.

It seemed it was up to her to make the first move.

"Good evening Jonas, it's lovely to meet you," she began with forced cheer and borrowed confidence. Had he been in her class at the village school? None of them looked familiar, yet they were her age, so they must have been there. How could she have completely forgotten all these people? She held out her hand to shake his, and he grasped it, then dropped it in panic and blushed beet red, before bowing so low he almost fell over.

Trying to hide her smile, she touched his shoulder gently. "There's no need to stand on ceremony, please. I'm Astrid. And I'd love to know all of your names."

Jonas finally gathered enough composure to look her in the eye, and grinned a lopsided grin. "Hello Astrid, I'm very pleased to meet you too. We've always wondered if the Queen had a child, and what you would be like, and we're all so happy to be here."

He went around the group, telling her their names, until there was only one person left.

A tall girl in a long green dress stepped forward and extended her hand, and Astrid froze. Her hair was swept into an elegant updo, but there was no mistaking its pure white colour, or the girl's pretty face. They'd been seared into Astrid's brain when the memory had returned at that awful breakfast with her mother. This was her friend, the one who had gifted her the book. Who had stayed over with her in the castle, giggling all night and trading confidences, perhaps. She wanted so badly for that to have been true – but all she knew for sure was that this was the person she'd hurt so badly with her still-mysterious and uncontrollable powers.

"And this is Emilja," Jonas said.

Astrid forced herself to step forward, say hello and shake her hand, despite her trembling legs and sweaty palms. Could this girl be her friend again, or would she subconsciously hate her, even though she'd never know why?

"Are you interested in a tour of the castle?" she asked nervously. "Or we could just stay here, of course…"

Bright-eyed Kye stepped forward. "We'd love to explore! We've always wondered what it looked like on the inside." He stopped abruptly, and blushed furiously. "Not to be nosy or anything…"

Pushing down her disquiet, Astrid grinned. "You can be as nosy as you like." Excitement bubbled up within her. She hadn't been this happy since, well, long before she could remember. There were people her age in the desolate, bleak old castle. Potential friends. "Come on!"

For more than an hour they traipsed along the corridors, peeking into empty rooms, sneaking into bedchambers, shuffling through hidden tunnels, and huffing and puffing up and down draughty spiral staircases. Always Astrid was conscious of where Emilja was, glancing at her out of the corner of her eye, and listening carefully whenever she spoke, each word a jewel that brought back memories of their friendship. Nights they'd spent right here, tiptoeing along the cold stone floors, slipping out to the stables to spend time with the horses, or exploring the newly remembered portrait gallery that contained all those strangely happy paintings of her with her once-loving mother.

When they clattered their way up the narrow stairs to the roof, she smiled to see the delight in Emilja's eyes as she looked out over the valley, and Astrid glowed as she suddenly recalled nights they'd camped out up here, staring at the stars as they whispered their hopes and dreams to each other. How had she forgotten all of that? *Any* of that? How had Emilja?

Later the neatly dressed but motley crew traipsed through the kitchen, and the scent of freshly baked bread triggered memories of visits Astrid had made to Emilja's house, and the joy she'd felt crammed into the small cottage alongside all of the girl's brothers and sisters. The sense of belonging when her friend's mother had hugged her. The noise and warmth and love there in that tiny cottage had been such a stark contrast to the silence and isolation of Astrid's life in the castle.

Tears pricked her eyes as she lamented the loss of their friendship, but she hoped tonight would be the first step to getting it back. Prayed that the spell would hold, and Emilja would never remember what she'd done to her.

When Jonas murmured that he couldn't possibly climb another staircase, Astrid's aching feet were relieved, and she cheerfully led them back to the Blue Room, where they ate a feast fit for a queen. Astrid's distress and guilt at how hungry they all were soon gave way to joy, and she lapped up every word the teenagers spoke as they chatted amongst themselves about life in the village, and whose sibling had recently married, or gone off on an adventure to find work, or in search of a far-away romance. She felt included, the glow of the golden candlelight and the warmth of their conversation wrapping her in kind-hearted comfort.

When they recovered their strength, they headed back to the ballroom and danced, their laughter infectious as they swirled each other around the sparkling room. There were seven girls and six guys in the group, so towards the end of the night Astrid found herself dancing a slow waltz with Emilja.

"I'm so happy you all came tonight," she murmured. "I hope you'll want to spend more time here. We could have so much fun."

The girl in the green dress smiled. "It's been wonderful, thank you for inviting us."

A lock of her white hair came loose from her bun and swept across her forehead, and Astrid lifted it gently out of her eyes and tucked it behind her ear. "You have such glorious hair. So unusual."

The other girl frowned as Astrid's fingers grazed her cheek. "It wasn't always like this. It used to be deep red apparently, but I was ill a few years ago, and my mother said it changed my hair overnight. Everyone teases me and calls me the Snow Queen –" She broke off, and a shadow crossed her face.

Stomach clenching in fear, Astrid gulped in a nervous breath. She knew people called her mother the Snow Queen. Did this mean the villagers suspected there was a link to what had happened to Emilja?

Please no.

She wanted so desperately for them to be friends again, for this girl to come up to the castle for sleepovers like she used to. She wanted them *all* to be her friends, and it saddened her that the villagers took the bonds they shared with each other so for granted. Her lonely heart ached as she watched the easy companionship between them, and she yearned to spend time with people her own age too, the way they all did. To know she had someone to experience things with, the joys and the challenges, the good times and the bad. Someone to understand her.

When the music finished, she returned to the group with Emilja, and joined in as they all raised their glasses in a toast, beaming at her as they thanked her for their magical evening in a faery tale castle. The warmth of their appreciation and enthusiasm washed over her, and as she basked in their attention, she finally relaxed. They seemed happy to be in her company, happy to include her in their circle of conversation.

Kye poured out the last drops from the jug of spiced punch and pouted, and Astrid smiled at him. "Don't worry, I'll have them bring more."

Sauntering off to find a servant to rustle up additional refreshments, she grinned. She was thirsty too, from all the dancing, and all the chatter, but her eyes were sparkling, and warmth and comfort and deepest joy wrapped around her as she spoke to the castle steward. The whole world looked different now, glittering with the potential of real friendship, and an end to the loneliness that had for so long shrouded her days.

Chapter 5

It took a long time for Astrid to return to her new friends. People kept pressing close to her, introducing themselves as her mother's loyal subjects, remarking on her striking similarity to the Queen, and begging for favours in areas she had no clue about. Trapped in conversations she struggled to extricate herself from, she tried to be polite, to sound intelligent, to convey warmth instead of her mother's icy chill.

Despite her best efforts, she was drowning. She was in way over her head, but had to admit it was gratifying that the glamorous guests were so intrigued by her, and wanted so desperately to meet her. Moment by moment she gained a little more confidence, and she was fascinated that so many of them still cast nervous glances at where the Queen sat alone on her throne on the dais, elevated above the rest of the room.

"I'm so sorry about your father," someone said softly from behind her, and Astrid spun around in shock. No one ever mentioned her father to her. Certainly not her mother.

"Thank you, I guess," she murmured. Her mind whirred. She'd never met her father, never even seen a portrait of him. And she'd never seen this woman before either. "Did you know him?"

Inclining her head regally, the stranger smiled. She was tall and elegant, her eyes sparkling like sapphires. Was she a friend of her mother's? Ruler of a neighbouring kingdom?

"I knew them both, back before they met." The woman paused, then arched one perfect brow. "I was in love with him, but then I foolishly introduced him to my best friend."

Her eyes glittered icily, and the lines around her mouth deepened, harsh with pain as she remembered. For a moment she looked exactly like the Queen – the same severity to her expression, the same sadness.

Astrid shivered. "My mother?"

"Yes, your mother was once my best friend. And, well, let's just say, we may have had a fight over him. Even though I'd told her I liked him. Even though he liked me first. I was certain she'd cast some terrible spell on him, to force him to choose her."

Astrid's face drained of colour and her palms tingled. The image of Emilja's triumphant expression when the boy Astrid liked had asked her out instead slammed into her mind, quickly followed by the vision of her unleashing her icy powers on her friend, freezing her skin, piercing her heart, and turning her vibrant red hair bright, stark white.

Was she just as evil as her mother?

"What happened?" she whispered, horrified, yet desperate to know more.

"Well, your mother was queen, and she had certain… unnatural powers. What choice did I have? I knew he would never settle for me, not when he could have her.

When she was determined that he would be hers. So I fled. I hid myself away in a cottage in the woods, trying to come to terms with the betrayal."

Astrid winced. She wanted to escape back to her chamber. To hide, from her mother, from the guests, from her new friends, from this stranger. From everyone and everything that reminded her of the awful thing she'd done.

The woman smiled sadly. "It wasn't true though."

"What?" Astrid's voice came out as a squeak, confusion making her sway unsteadily in her increasingly uncomfortable high heels.

"Edvard did love your mother. And he'd never loved me. That was just wishful thinking on my part." Her voice broke, and Astrid knew deep within herself the physical pain and grief of this revelation. Remembered how she'd felt when the boy she liked had chosen Emilja.

"How did you –"

The woman grimaced. "I just found out. I guess you could say that a little bird told me. And that's why I came tonight, to make amends. To apologise to the Queen."

The castle steward approached them, wariness in his eyes. "Darja."

She barely glanced at him, just enough to take in his uniform and nod politely, before she turned back to Astrid.

"As I was saying –"

But the steward had caught Astrid's attention, and he beckoned her away. "Your guests are waiting for you."

"Oh my gosh, yes!" She turned back to the woman who was gazing at her with such sad eyes. The candles in the nearest sconce flickered, as though a ghost had come too close, and for just a moment in their shifting light, the woman looked lost. Her dress was more ragged than Astrid had realised, her face was smudged with... dirt? And were they leaves in her hair? "It was lovely to meet you... Darja? I'm sorry about my mother... Well, um..."

And she fled, her mind spinning with thoughts of her mysterious father, and the possibility that her mother wasn't as terrible as she'd always thought. That somewhere in their past she had loved her daughter. That once upon a time mother and child had been happy in their life together, as the paintings she'd discovered so vividly implied.

That her father had loved her mother.

Had the grief at losing him turned the widowed wife into the Snow Queen? Did being with her daughter cause her pain because she represented her lost love, and was that what had turned her bitter and cruel?

Astrid wanted to find the woman and ask her more questions, but the disclosures had left her reeling, her head spinning, and for now she was relieved to return to the safety of her new friends.

When she rejoined them they were all talking together, voices heated, but they all broke off when they noticed her, and all their eyes, as one, turned on her.

"Thank you so much for coming tonight, it's been wonderful," Astrid said, filling her glass from one of the new jugs the steward had delivered. "And I hope you'll all return again. I think there will be another ball next Friday. Not that tonight is over yet, of course!"

For the first time, she didn't feel anxious about time repeating. Not if these new friends would be part of her life, trapped in the time loop with her. She grinned as they lifted their glasses in a toast to her.

"To Astrid," Jonas began. "May you always be steady of foot and on the same level."

What?

Pain seared up her left leg, and Astrid blinked against a new memory – herself at fifteen, running down the school's hall, Jonas lounging against the lockers, then sticking his foot out into her path so she fell, landing in an awkward heap and breaking her left ankle.

How had she forgotten that? And what had she done to warrant such nastiness? She heard his voice in her head echoing from that day: "You think you're so far above us Princess Prissy Pants, but it's time for you to come back down to our level."

One of the girls, Vika, raised her glass next. "May your head always remain clear."

Astrid's temple started to throb, and she winced as she recalled a ball game where a younger version of this girl had thrown the ball right at her head, hard, when she missed a shot.

She hadn't meant to miss it, so why had Vika been so mean to her? Then she heard the girl's long-ago voice: "You're so selfish Astrid, you should have thrown the ball to me. But no, you just want all the attention and all the praise for yourself. Don't you know what being part of a team means?"

Distressed, but unable to move away or defend herself, Astrid lifted tear-filled eyes to the rest of the group, praying there weren't any more accusations coming.

But Kye lifted his glass, and a dagger of pain shot through her knee. "May you always keep your balance Astrid," he grinned, and she saw long ago him pushing her over on the village skating rink, then laughing at her tears.

"You're always pushing in, always thinking you're better than us," the younger Kye shouted in her memory, his face red with scorn. "We think you should push off back to your fancy castle!"

And then Emilja stepped forward, and Astrid's heart shattered like glass. "And may you always know who your friends are, and never be stabbed in the back."

Astrid cried out in bewilderment, and agony, as the sensation of a knife piercing her back rippled through her. When the memory came this time, her knees buckled and she staggered awkwardly before clutching the arm of a chair to stay upright. She'd confided in her friend how much she liked the boy, and Emilja had said she'd ask him to the dance for her. But when he came over with a rose and asked Emilja, not Astrid, to be his date, her friend had laughed. "Oops, sorry! I accidentally told him that you *didn't* like him, so now he's mine."

Astrid remembered the white-hot rage that had swept through her at her friend's betrayal. Remembered shouting: "No, he's mine!"

And remembered the fear and confusion on Emilja's face when the jagged shards of ice formed between them and pointed straight at her heart. Saw her raising her arms in supplication. Begging her not to hurt her. Promising she could have the boy. Apologising for her treachery.

It was too late though. Astrid hadn't been able to rein in the mysterious power and stop herself.

But the furious Emilja standing before her tonight was not like the apologetic memory version. She was strong, and unrelenting, and fired up with wrath.

"I never understood how an illness could turn my hair white, but there seemed to be no other explanation. Then a few days ago your mother came down to the village with invitations, the first time in years she'd bothered to show her face, and I started getting flashes of memory, of a daughter from the castle, of a world filled with sunshine and blue skies. It didn't make sense – we weren't aware that she had any children, and yet, somehow I did know. And while I thought the world had never been anything but grey and threatening, I could picture a blue sky, could smell the perfume of springtime flowers."

"I've dreamed of that too," Astrid whispered.

Emilja's eyes flashed with anger, and accusation. "I don't know what you did to us, what your mother did, but when you went to get more drinks that woman came to talk to us." She gestured at Darja, who was watching them from the other side of the ballroom. "And we all started remembering things. Remembering *you*."

An icy chill raced up Astrid's spine, and she staggered under the weight of their fury. "But that's not true," she whispered, voice anguished. "Darja came here to apologise, she told me so herself. And you apologised to me too Emilja, because *you* betrayed *me*." Tears were filling her eyes, but she sternly willed them not to fall.

The white-haired girl ignored her words and kept ranting. "You're so entitled! He wasn't going to like you just because you wanted him to. How could you not realise that? He chose me because he liked *me*, not because I stole him away from you. Yet you destroyed me, and made me look like an old woman. Made all of us feel inferior with your showing off and your wilful ignorance."

Emilja glared at her. "We hate you," she spat. "So stay up here in your castle, all alone, and never talk to us again."

And she turned on her heel and stormed out, all the other villagers rushing in her wake. What had Darja told them? And why?

Devastated, Astrid sank to the floor, and when her mother stood up on the dais and invited everyone to the winter solstice ball the following Friday, she couldn't find it in herself to care. Maybe she deserved an eternity of winter, a lifetime without warmth, or friends, or love. Maybe this twisted time loop was her fate.

Or her curse.

Chapter 6

A rumble of thunder jolted Astrid awake, and she sat up abruptly, clutching the heavy quilts around her and rubbing her eyes against the white glare of the outside world. When she remembered what had happened at the ball the night before, she sank back down and pulled the covers over her head. She couldn't face the day, couldn't face the world. Couldn't face her life.

How had she managed to hurt her friend? What power did she have? Sitting up again, she stared at her hands. They looked normal. She flicked her left hand towards the curtains, expecting shards of ice to tear them to pieces, or some form of electricity to singe them, but nothing happened. She tried her other hand. Still nothing. Taking a deep breath, she tried to focus.

"Come on," she muttered. "Show me what you can do. Do your worst, I dare you." She held up both hands, like she had in the horrifying memory, and waited for a flicker of light, a crash of jagged hailstones, even a single drop of water. But still nothing happened.

Movement at the door caught her eye, and she quickly hid her hands under the covers.

"Good morning," the Queen said imperiously. "Did you enjoy yourself last night? It looked like you and your friends had a wonderful time."

Fury shot through Astrid, and her palms tingled. She stuffed them under her thighs and prayed, ironically, that they wouldn't start shooting arrows of ice now.

"They hated me. And they were as mean to me last night as when I was at school. Why did you make me forget how awful they were to me? They bullied me terribly, and I have no idea why. Was it because of you?" she demanded.

"I didn't –"

Astrid ignored her, and blundered on. "But even worse, I don't know what you did to them to make them forget the past, or how they started remembering it – but they do remember, and they *despise* me. They never want to see me again. Are you happy now, Mother?"

The Queen bustled into the chamber, her skirts swirling around her, and lowered herself onto her daughter's bed. "Of course I'm not happy, how could you think that? I wanted you to have friends. I thought they'd forgotten what happened."

Astrid's frozen heart felt like it was breaking, shattering within her chest, the jagged pieces splintering off to pierce her organs. "So you had to cast another spell on them to make them want to come and spend time with me? You tricked them into thinking they liked me?" she whispered. Then she laughed, although even she could hear it was bordering on hysteria. "But even your magic wasn't strong enough to convince them. They remembered that they hated me, and they hate me still."

"It's not like that," her mother said defensively.

"What else could it be?" Astrid demanded, then stopped abruptly. "Wait, who's Darja?"

The Queen's face paled, and for a split-second she struggled to compose herself. Then her expression smoothed back to its usual mask, icy and remote. "I don't know anyone by that name," she said stiffly.

"Right," Astrid snapped, her eyes blazing with fury. "Just get out. Go and do whatever you do, wherever you do it. I hate my life, and I hate you too!"

The Queen looked as though she wanted to argue, then her shoulders dropped and she shook her head. "I'm sorry you feel that way. I have to leave for work, but I'll be back soon, and we can talk some more. And I'll have a lovely surprise for you, I promise."

"Get out!" Astrid screamed. And once she was totally alone again, she finally succumbed to her tears.

Time dragged on after that, the next few days creeping slowly by as Astrid stayed in her room and sulked. Kristina came by at mealtimes, with trays of delicious smelling food and luscious desserts, but she couldn't tempt Astrid to eat a bite, or even to speak.

It crushed her to realise that her former schoolmates had hated her before she wounded Emilja. They'd been cruel to her from the very beginning, tripping her over, tormenting her in class, physically harming her, making fun of her whenever they could. She'd thought she was miserable here, stuck away in the castle, all alone, but it turned out she'd been even more unhappy before that, when she'd been surrounded by people, by classmates, by supposed friends, every day.

Why had they hated her? What had she ever done to them? Shards of ice pierced her heart all over again, and she sobbed out her confusion and pain.

Yet there *had* been a time when she and Emilja were friends. As they'd all walked the corridors the other night, she'd *remembered* happy occasions. They'd had sleepovers, in the castle as well as at Emilja's home; had climbed up to the roof to look at the stars, and spent time in the stables with the horses. And they'd been friends at school too – the memory of her hurting Emilja had begun with them climbing the school steps together, laughing and happy.

Where was that faery tale book Emilja had given her, with its sweet inscription and beautiful illustrations? It was proof that she wasn't losing her mind. Proof that they'd been close friends. That she'd been liked once. Had cared for someone, and been cared for in turn. Had laughed with a companion, carefree and close, confiding secrets and sharing dreams.

Desperately Astrid searched her bookshelf, then her desk. She rummaged through her wardrobe, then sank to her knees on the cold stone floor and peered under her bed, plunging her hand into the darkness as she tried to find the confirmation that she hadn't always been despised. But there was nothing there either.

Depressed, she curled up in the window seat and stared out at the monotonous white snow, weeping tears of frustration and despair. Her life stretched out before her, as cold and unforgiving as the bleak landscape, and she wondered how she would find the strength to continue her miserable existence. Maybe she would have to demand her mother cast another spell, a better spell, to wipe her own mind of what had happened, as well as everyone else's.

When Kristina tried to tempt her with dinner that night, Astrid shook her head at the steaming tray, then jumped up and clutched her arm.

"Do you know where the book is?" she implored.

Her maid stared at her blankly.

"The one from Emilja, from years ago. You know, the gift she gave me after staying here one weekend."

"I don't know anything about a book, my lady."

Trying to hide her impatience, Astrid gestured to her bed, then to the space beneath it. "But I told you about it the night you slept here, with me."

Eyes widening in surprise, Kristina stared at her aghast, clearly unsettled by her claim. "I've never stayed in here, my lady!" she replied indignantly. "I sleep in the servant quarters. I would never presume!"

Astrid felt she was going mad. "But you did. The night after the ball, when I screamed as the clock struck midnight and the date flipped backwards. You got me to my chamber before my mother could reprimand me, and you were so cold, and I was so worried, that I asked you to stay. I told you about the book Emilja gave me, and you shared with me that Cook was concerned about the eternal winter too, that our food was running out, and we both wondered if we were trapped in some kind of strange time loop."

"I'm sorry my lady, but I don't know what you're talking about." And, fear twisting her features into a frown, Kristina dropped the tray onto a small side table, then turned and hurried out of the room.

Thoughts racing wildly, Astrid paced around her chamber, tying herself in knots as she did her best to puzzle it out. Was she losing her mind? Was she inventing scenarios that just weren't true? But why would she do that?

Or had the spell her mother cast started to come undone, or run out altogether, leaving some people with their memories, and others still blissfully unaware?

On the fourth day, the Queen barged into Astrid's room without knocking, and demanded she get dressed immediately and meet her in the dining room for lunch. "And bathe first, please," she sniffed, wrinkling her nose.

Resigned, Astrid dragged herself out of bed and into her bathing room, where a relieved Kristina filled the tub then went to choose something suitable for her to wear. Sighing as the maid laced her into a blue dress, she studiously avoided her eyes in the mirror. Was the Queen going to punish her for her recent outburst? She'd never raised her voice to her mother before, never told her that she hated her, but she supposed it didn't matter – she couldn't get any more miserable than she already was.

Before, she'd ached with loneliness, yet had managed to remain hopeful that things would change when she could go out into the world and find her own place in it. But now she knew she was despised by everyone who had ever met her, and the faith she'd had for a future filled with friendship and maybe even love fractured within her. Gulping in a desperate breath, she tried to steel herself to cope with the solitary existence that stretched out before her.

When she stumbled into the dining room, Astrid opened her mouth to question her mother, then froze when she saw a stranger standing at the window, gazing out over the ice-covered wasteland that surrounded the castle.

At her footsteps, he spun around, face rigid with fear.

Chapter 7

He sighed with relief. "You must be Astrid."

Blinking rapidly, she stared in wonder as he crossed the room to her. It was the guy from her dream, the one she'd been walking along the beach with. The one who'd been holding her hand. The one she'd been longing to kiss.

He was her age, or close to it, with wavy dark hair and dreamy emerald green eyes she wanted to dive right into. He was handsome, she supposed, definitely more appealing than the village boys, but it was the kindness of his expression, and his openness and lack of guile that made him so attractive. She was still smarting from the daggers the teenagers at the ball had torn her heart apart with.

"Um, yes, I'm Astrid... I just, well, uh, who are you?" She groaned at her clumsy reply, but he just smiled.

"Don't be afraid, I'm a friend. Well, I will be..." He winced. "I hope!"

It made her giggle that he seemed almost as awkward as she was, and her body softened as the tension drained from her.

Taking her hand, he bent low over it, almost bowing, then gazed up at her with those eyes. Thickly lashed, sparkling with intelligence and wit, and twinkling with mischief as well.

"I hope so too," she said, then her forehead scrunched. Was she supposed to know his name? "Um, sorry, have we already been introduced?"

Before he could reply, her mother swept into the room, and the stranger dropped her hand and sprang backwards. Astrid's shoulders slumped in disappointment.

"Good, I see that you've met Finn," the Queen announced imperiously. "He will be staying with us for a while, so I expect you to show him around, teach him about the kingdom's history, and keep him entertained and out of my way."

Baffled, Astrid nodded her acceptance. She didn't remember them ever having a guest at the castle, and couldn't imagine why he was the first. She opened her mouth to ask one of the many questions buzzing around in her brain, but her mother interrupted again.

"I'll see you both at the ball on Friday night. Behave yourselves," she commanded. Then, with an imperious glance at each of them, she waltzed out of the room.

Cheeks flaming with embarrassment, Astrid wished the floor would break apart and swallow her whole, but she had no such luck. One of the kitchen maids came in with a luncheon feast, and she resigned herself to her fate.

"I apologise for my mother," she began, as they watched the girl pour warm apple cider spiced with cinnamon into two glasses. "She can be quite... abrupt."

Finn took a gulp of the warm sweet brew, closed his eyes for a moment in satisfaction, then opened them and shook his head. "You have nothing to be sorry for. She's perfectly charming."

"No one's ever described her that way before, but okay," Astrid replied doubtfully, then peered at him, puzzled. "How did you meet her anyway? And why would you come here, of all places. Sick of all the sunshine where you live?"

For a moment his smile slipped, and he gazed off somewhere over her shoulder, perplexed. Then he rallied. Taking another sip of the warm cider, his eyes cleared, and he turned all his attention back to Astrid.

"I've never been to a castle before, so this is an adventure. And your mother kindly offered the use of her library – *your* library – for a project I'm working on, and I couldn't resist. She also said you'd be able to help me." He stopped, panicked. "If you're not too busy! I don't want to impose."

Astrid picked listlessly at the roast vegetables on her plate and tried not to reveal just how desperately happy she was to have a task. Her days stretched out emptily before her, without purpose or joy. Talking to the villagers the other night had highlighted how lonely she was, how trapped she felt, and how deeply meaningless her existence was. Her life was filled with lessons she had no interest in, working towards qualifications she didn't need. What was the point of anything?

"Hey, are you okay?" Finn asked, reaching across the table to touch her hand. "I'll stay out of your hair if you don't have time for me, you don't have to feel bad about being too busy. I really don't want to be a bother."

The feather-light touch of his fingers on her skin sent heat radiating up Astrid's arm. Her heart raced, and she suddenly wanted to cry. No doubt Finn would turn against her too, use her for whatever project he was doing, then laugh in her face and walk out the door the minute it was done, leaving her more alone that ever.

She didn't think she could cope with another rejection, even from a stranger. It would definitely be best to stay away from him. She opened her mouth to refuse, but he spoke before she could.

"It must be so lonely for you here," he added, as though reading her thoughts. "Cut off from the rest of the world, with your mother away so often for work. What do you do Astrid? Who do you talk to?"

The compassion in his voice nearly broke her. No one had ever worried about how she felt, or wondered what she thought, or how she spent her days. Especially not her mother, who only cared about herself, her constant travels and her endless winter balls.

Surreptitiously wiping away the tear welling in her eye, she forced a bright smile. "I spend most of my time on my lessons, with my tutors, so I primarily speak to them."

"Ah, so you're brainy. What do you want to do when you finish studying?"

"Well, um…" She trailed off. No one had ever asked her what she wanted before either. What did she plan to do with her life? She'd been too listless to care. Would she stay here, living with her distant mother, or move away and go to university somewhere? Maybe she could get a job in a bookstore in a faraway town, so she could read all day, free of the oppressive presence of the castle and the ridiculous expectations of her mother? Mortified, she realised she didn't know enough people to even know what careers were possible. Or if she'd be allowed to have one.

Maybe she could pick Finn's brain. "What do you plan to do?" she asked him.

"Well, my grandmother assumes I'll take over the family business. My parents ran a store in my home town, and Gran has been overseeing it until I'm old enough, but I dream of doing more than that with my life." His eyes sparkled with passion, and his enthusiasm was infectious.

Astrid stared at him, willing him to continue. "What's your dream?"

"My friend thinks I should be an artist, because I love painting more than anything in the world, but I need to be practical. It has to be something that will earn me a living so I can support my gran."

He gazed wistfully at the painting above the fireplace, and Astrid stared at it too. She'd never paid any attention to it before, but it was beautiful, all golden summer light and green meadows. And was that her and her mother in the distance, holding hands? How had she never noticed the figures before, especially after so recently seeing all the portraits in the gallery? Perplexed, she wanted to rush over and peer at it, but she could examine a painting any day. Right now she was torn between jealousy that Finn had supportive people in his life, and the romantic notion of being an artist.

"Are there people who just paint?" she asked, then blushed at her stupidity. If there were paintings, obviously there were people who painted them.

But Finn smiled gently. "It's a good question. I've never met anyone who paints to make a living, I've only ever seen it as a hobby. Can you imagine though, getting to do what you love every day? To bring joy and beauty to people, and be able to feed yourself and your family with the proceeds." His eyes were shining, as though he was lit up from within, and she envied him with every fibre of her being.

"I love that idea too," she said shyly. "So will you paint while you're here?"

A blank look crossed his face, then his brow furrowed. Inhaling sharply, he shook his head. "I didn't bring any paints or brushes with me. I didn't bring much of anything, to be honest."

He looked confused again, but Astrid didn't notice, suddenly excited. A thread of memory was bubbling up, of a room in the castle filled with easels and canvases, and drawers filled with pigments in every colour imaginable. She could help him. Pushing her plate away, she leapt up from the table and walked towards him. "That doesn't matter, we have everything you'll need right here. Come on, I'll show you the art room."

She smiled bashfully. "I used to love painting I think, but I suppose I had no aptitude, because I can't remember the last time I did it. So you can use it all. There are shelves full of paints, stacks of blank canvases, everything you'll need. And there's a bedchamber right next to it, so you can stay in that one. I'll have Kristina make it up for you."

Reaching for his hand, she dragged him out of the room and up the stairs, and he laughed sweetly at her eagerness. When they reached the second floor though, Astrid suddenly became acutely aware of her actions, and dropped his hand in embarrassment.

"I'm sorry, I got carried away," she said, cheeks aflame. "I didn't mean to drag you off before you even got to finish your lunch."

He shrugged, then grinned at her. "It's fine, I ate enough. I'd love to see the art room."

"Okay." She tried to pull herself together, and to calm down and sound coherent at least. "It's just down here."

She couldn't recall the last time she'd been in the art room, or why she'd stopped going. Why had her mother enspelled her to forget painting too? There was something painful there, but it drifted just out of reach, tormenting her. Forcing a smile, she opened the door to the studio and gestured for him to enter. When she followed him inside, her gasp was as loud as his.

Paintings took up every wall, with others stacked in the corners. Incredible landscapes of enchanted woodland glades covered in wildflowers and butterflies, with beautiful faeries dancing in golden streams of sunlight. Mountains soaring heavenward under rainbows that arched through vivid blue skies, illuminating waterfalls into cascades of shimmering jewels. Stunning ice worlds inhabited by mysterious snow beings. Ancient forests tangled in gowns of ivy, with tiny creatures peeking out from the boles of trunks and in the sweet little homes they'd made in the twining root systems.

Then there were the portraits, of people who looked like they were stepping out of a doorway from hundreds of years ago, contrasted with the students from the village – kids she didn't remember ever seeing until the ball the other night. Each face was exquisitely captured, the eyes sparkling with amusement, or hooded with hidden depths of sorrow. So much emotion, so much depth, that the artist must have known them well, and have spent a lot of time with each one.

Finn paused at a canvas that depicted Astrid and Emilja, lounging on a colourful blanket with a picnic basket between them, both of them laughing like they were the closest of friends. They looked so real and true that they might have glanced up at the two people staring at them and waved. Astrid's heart raced, adrenaline pumped through her body, and her throat tightened as she tried to swallow her distress at the image, and the astonishment at what it all meant.

"Who painted these?" Finn asked her, awestruck.

"I did." It was a whisper torn from deep within. "I mean, I don't remember doing it, and yet…" She clutched one hand to her chest. "I can feel the consistency as I mixed the paints, see each stroke of the brush as I added it to the surface, recall the emotions I channelled as I connected with their energy."

"And what about this one?" Finn pointed to a beautiful still-life of mistletoe, a wicked grin on his face. "Did you have anyone in mind when you painted it?"

Blushing scarlet, Astrid stared at the artwork. It must have been for the boy she and Emilja fought over. Had he been at the ball the other night? She couldn't recall his face, or his name, couldn't recall anything about him. Somehow all the most important aspects of her life were hidden in shadow, obscured by a fog so thick she couldn't pierce its mystery, yet all the pain she felt was for the loss of Emilja, not a potential boyfriend.

The shame she'd felt at the ball slammed back into her, and she shuddered as remnants of the pain in her body returned. Uncomfortable with the direction of their conversation, she gazed around the room again.

When her eyes alighted on a pile of blank canvases, she turned to Finn and smiled. "There you are, lots of surfaces for you to create on, and that cupboard over there has all the brushes, paints and other supplies." She remembered that. The scent of the paint, and the turpentine for cleaning. The jewel-bright hues of all the tubes of pigment.

While he exclaimed over all the art tools, there was a timid knock on the door, and Kristina poked her head in.

"Do you need a hand in here, my lady, or shall I set up the bedchamber?"

"We're fine," Astrid said curtly, disappointed by the interruption. Then her voice softened. "But if you could set up Finn's room, that would be wonderful. And after that you'll need to clear all these paintings out of here and throw them –" she began, but Finn clutched her arm.

"Don't move them," he begged her. "I want to spend time studying them."

The thought made her blush again, as though he would be able to see inside her soul if he gazed at them too long, but she nodded reluctantly and turned back to the maid. "Okay then, you can just make up the chamber next door."

Kristina curtseyed and left the room. When Astrid turned back to her guest, he was staring at her as though trying to drink in every detail of her. "I want to paint you," he blurted out, then smiled bashfully. "Sorry, I mean, if that would be all right?"

A quiver of nervous anticipation rippled through her body, and butterflies danced in her belly. "Maybe."

"The movement of your hair, the way your eyes sparkle in the light and reflect the colours of the canvases, everything about you is just so... So perfect."

Astrid blushed again, flustered, which made him smile impishly. Who was this guy? She tried to get a handle on her discomfort, prayed the heat would leave her cheeks. "I should give you the tour first though, right? Show you where everything you'll need is?"

"Of course," Finn said, and laughed, a gentle, kind laugh. He was nothing like the boys from the other night.

"I'm just so excited to start painting again. I haven't felt that in a long time. Promise me that you'll sit for me."

Shrugging helplessly, Astrid nodded, then wondered what she'd gotten herself into. Keeping him at arm's length was going to be even harder now.

Chapter 8

Astrid had never thought much about her home or its history, having nothing to compare it to, but as she showed Finn around the castle, she found herself loving every icy stone inch of its gloomy corridors. His awe as he drank it all in warmed her heart, and seeing it through his eyes gave her new perspective. The connection to it she'd always denied clicked into place, a connection that linked her cold, empty heart to its cold, empty, echoing rooms. The thought should have scared her, but it didn't. She loved it. It gave her strength. A sense of power and control. She was as cold and remote as its oldest stones, and she needed no one and no thing to survive.

Climbing the narrow spiral staircase to the rooftop, a ribbon of guilt wove around her heart as she remembered taking Emilja and the other villagers up there the other night, but she pushed her hurt down. They meant nothing to her now. She'd hardened her heart to them, to everyone.

Well, maybe not *everyone*, because when she pushed open

the door and heard Finn sigh with pleasure, her heart fluttered a little, and a smile lit up her face as she watched his child-like delight.

"This is so beautiful," he cried, running from one side of the rooftop to the other, exclaiming at the breathtaking views out over the snow-blanketed valleys and up to the remote and icy mountain peaks. "We have to come up here to paint, please," he implored her.

She giggled, stirred by his enthusiasm. "Sure." Then she noticed how badly he was shivering. "But not right now. You're going to need far warmer clothes for that. Why don't I show you the library, and we can sit by the fire with a mug of hot chocolate while you tell me what you're researching."

They spent the rest of the day sprawled out on comfy old leather couches in the massive library, Finn reading about the history of the region and its politics, Astrid engrossed in a novel between maths and geography sessions, and feeling a surprising level of comfort with this stranger.

For the next two days, snow swirled blizzard-strong outside, and they holed up in the library in front of the roaring flames, alternating her lessons and his research with long conversations about their lives. The more they spoke, the more of her memories were unlocked, and there were several moments where she had to fight the dizziness as they crashed back over her.

There were good memories and bad – friendship then loneliness, motherly love then remoteness, joy then fear. It was all bottled up tightly within her, so overwhelming it made her head spin, but Finn's kindness and empathy thawed something within her, and she found herself telling him things she'd never imagined sharing with a single soul.

And her confidences inspired his own. Both had lost a parent young, Astrid her father in a hiking accident before she was born, Finn his mother when he was just a toddler, which had sent his father off to join the navy and left him essentially orphaned, brought up by his grandmother.

"I'm so sorry," Astrid whispered, shyly reaching out to touch his hand in comfort. When he turned his over and gently grasped hers, she bit her lip, desperately trying to stifle a gasp and remain calm. Yet her heart was racing, her face was flushed, and goosebumps covered her arms. Excitement thrummed through her veins, and she gazed into his eyes as anticipation and desire flooded her body.

"Astrid, I –"

Whatever he was going to say was cut off when her mother flung open the heavy wooden doors. As they crashed against the wall, the candles in the room flickered, and sparks flew from the fire.

"Good, there you both are. The ball will begin at eight o'clock tonight, and food will be served, so we won't meet for dinner beforehand. Finn, there's a suit in your wardrobe to wear, and Astrid, I expect you to make an effort."

The Queen glowered at her daughter, who wilted under her gaze, then slammed the door behind her as she stormed off. Two of the candles were snuffed out and the fire faded to embers, as though all the warmth in the room had been sucked from it by the Snow Queen.

Astrid turned stiffly to her companion, her head already teeming with images of herself tripping on her long dress, falling down the stairs, or spilling a drink on one of her mother's guests. "I suppose we should go and get ready," she said, regret in her voice and her eyes. "Shall I send someone to help you dress?"

Frowning, Finn shook his head, and Astrid cursed her stupidity. Normal people didn't have servants. He must think she was so stuck up. But as he tidied the pile of books he'd been reading and gathered his notes, he smiled at her. "I'll be fine. I'll see you back down here at five to eight?"

"Okay," she said, then raced out of the room and up the stairs to her chamber before she could say anything else to embarrass herself.

Flinging herself onto her bed, she pulled a pillow over her head to muffle her squeals. She could still feel the warmth of his hand as he'd cradled hers, see the compassion in his eyes as he'd listened so intently to everything she said. Could he possibly like her? Did she like him? Or was she just so starved of company, and attention, that she would latch on to anyone who spoke kindly to her?

Then a hot surge of shame burned her skin. How could she have assumed he'd need a servant to get dressed? That look on his face when she'd offered, was it disappointment in his frown? Condescension? And why did she need assistance? Was she so pathetic that she couldn't get some clothes on without help?

Determined to do things for herself, she rose to her feet, but when her door opened and Kristina stepped lightly inside, she allowed her maid to run a bath for her and pick out a gown, then spend more time than usual wrestling her hair into some semblance of order.

Finally she was ready. Heart hammering, she made her way downstairs to the library, and drew in a sharp breath. Finn was lounging against the wall in a midnight-blue suit, exuding elegance and sophistication, and a heat that radiated off him and threatened to burn her up. Trying to keep her hands steady, she slipped an arm through his, praying he couldn't hear the wild racing of her heart, see the blush covering her whole body, or sense the impact he was having on her physically and emotionally. Dizzy with hope and expectation, she led him into the ballroom.

The week before, she'd been too caught up in seeing the teenagers from the village to pay much attention to her surroundings, but now she followed Finn's gaze around the high-ceilinged space. A huge, freshly cut pine tree stood in one corner, illuminated with strings of faery lights and decorated with ropes of tinsel, bundles of cinnamon sticks, clove-studded oranges and hundreds of intricately carved Yule symbols. Near the raised platform where the imposing gold-draped throne stood, the chamber orchestra was warming up, and neatly dressed waiters circulated with trays of sparkling liquid in delicate glass flutes. Urns of flowers added their perfume to the pine tree's sweet scent, and the flames of hundreds of sandalwood candles flickered and danced in the warm air.

"It's so magical," Finn said, eyes wide with wonder.

Astrid smiled, relieved and happy that he still hadn't shrugged her arm away. Taking a deep breath, she gathered all her courage. "Would you like to dance?"

Sweeping a low bow, he murmured "of course", and drew her out onto the dance floor. He guided her effortlessly, gracefully, around the room, and she floated on a wave of joy, wrapped in the warmth and comfort of his embrace. Time stopped, then expanded, and when she peeked up at his face, he was haloed against the golden candlelight. Astrid was aware of every inch of her skin that pressed against him, every tingling nerve of her body, every sweet whirl of energy that bound them together.

When the Queen made her way to the front of the room,

Finn kept one arm around Astrid as they faced the dais, and she leaned into him, desperate to stay connected. "Are you all right?" he whispered, and all she could do was nod and smile, too overwhelmed by how right it felt to be so close to him to utter a coherent sentence.

"Welcome to the Yule ball." The Queen's voice boomed out over the crowd. There was a loud cheer, and the rustling of fabrics and shuffling of feet, before a respectful silence returned. "May this enchanted solstice evening bring you joy and rebirth, and light and hope in the darkness. Let the celebrations and the feasting begin!"

The small orchestra began another song, and half of the crowd stayed on the dance floor, while the other half made their way to the tables around the edges of the room.

"Hungry?" Astrid asked.

Finn's stomach growled, and he nodded sheepishly, cheeks stained red with embarrassment.

She led him to a small table in the corner of the vast room, away from the crowd, and they sat together, both mesmerised by their surroundings, the delicacies served up on fine china, all the colourful people swirling by them, and the enchantment of the night.

When their plates were cleared, Astrid took a big gulp of mead from her crystal glass, trying to summon some courage, and gazed at Finn. "Why did you stop painting?" she asked tentatively. "If that's not too personal?"

For a moment his eyes clouded with confusion, then he shrugged, feigning nonchalance. "It's hard to explain, but I think I was feeling trapped. My future was all mapped out – I would take over the store my parents had run, settle down with my childhood friend, never leave the house I was born in. There was no time for adventure or exploration.

No opportunity to choose anything. I'd never been beyond the mountain range that surrounds our village and cuts us off from the world, and I probably never would. But some part of me longed to escape. Longed for *more*."

He looked surprised by his own revelation, and screwed up his face, self-deprecating. "You must think I'm so selfish, wanting to run away and have fun while my poor, sweet grandmother needed me –"

"Not at all!" Astrid interjected, voice low and full of passion. "I totally understand what you mean. I've been feeling so trapped as well. Smothered by the boring inevitability of my life, the knowledge that I will never leave this castle. And I know I shouldn't complain," she said quickly. "I have no right, given my supposed faery-tale life and the blessings I should count, but I hate it here!"

She gasped, shocked that she'd admitted this out loud, and quickly looked around to check that she hadn't been overheard. "You must think I'm so spoiled and self-centred, complaining about living in a castle while so many people are living six to a room, struggling even to eat."

Finn smiled gently at her and shook his head. "Not at all. I think you're sweet and kind, and very considerate. You've given up all your time to help me, a total stranger."

While the compliment made her glow, Astrid knew she didn't deserve it. It wasn't her great altruism that made her spend so much time with Finn. It was pain and regret and deep loneliness – and the fact that she found him fascinating, charming and, yes, attractive, didn't hurt either.

Flustered, she knocked back the rest of her drink and looked around for another. Looked anywhere but at him.

"Hey," Finn said, reaching across the table and lifting her chin so their eyes met. His gaze was warm and tender.

"I'm grateful for your generous nature, and I treasure our growing friendship," he said, then stood and held out his hand. "Shall we dance again?"

Glowing at the praise, Astrid beamed at him, then placed her hand in his and let him lead her back out amongst the dancers, where they lost themselves in the rhythm of the music, the magic of the flickering candlelight and the heady scent of the flowers. Cheek resting on his shoulder, she imprinted the memory of how it felt to be in his arms deep into her heart, so it could sustain her when he inevitably left her.

Finally the clock inched towards midnight, and the Queen stood up from her throne. Finn jerked his chin in her direction, grinning at Astrid. "Pumpkin time?"

She giggled, then held her breath anxiously as her mother raised her arms. "Thank you so much for being here tonight everyone, it was wonderful to see you all, and to talk with you about how the season of ice and snow has been unfolding for you. And I very much hope you will all return next Friday night, for our winter solstice ball!"

Astrid's shoulders slumped, but Finn was laughing. "Awesome! Do you have balls like this every week? And does that mean there'll be another new suit in my wardrobe?" He looked so thrilled by the thought that Astrid swallowed down her fear and smiled back.

Besides, if he was going to stick around, being trapped in a time loop might not be such a terrible fate after all. With a wry grin, she wondered how many groundhog day solstice balls it would take her to figure out how to make Finn see her as more than just a friend.

Chapter 9

"So Finn, did you enjoy the ball?" the Queen asked, gaze piercing his soul.

They were sitting in the second-most formal dining room the next morning, the snow falling outside in a glaring white sheet that was making them all squint in the harsh light.

Heaping his plate with warm flaky pastries, Finn smiled. "Yes, Your Majesty. I've never attended anything like it before, or even dreamed of such a thing. It was wonderful. And thank you so much for the clothes, I would have been mortified to be the only one not suitably attired."

"I'm glad you enjoyed it."

"And there's another one next week, is that right? You didn't tell me that when we spoke." A frown creased his brow, and Astrid's heart clenched as his eyes clouded over with bewilderment.

The Queen poured him a coffee from the silver pot, and he automatically gulped half of it down, as though he was completely parched. His expression cleared, and he smiled as he set the fine china cup in its saucer and added cream and sugar to the remaining brew.

"And you dearest?" the Queen asked. "I assume you had a better time than last week."

Swallowing down her unrest with her own gulp of coffee, Astrid nodded. "Thank you Mother, I did."

"Wonderful." The Queen stood. "Well then, I have business to attend to, so I will leave you two to your day."

And she swept out, furs swishing around her ankles. When the door closed behind her, the room warmed a few degrees, and the intensity of the blinding white snow from outside eased. Astrid and Finn both relaxed and stopped squinting. Their muscles unclenched and their breathing became calmer, and Finn bit into one of the pastries, unconcerned by all the crumbs sprinkling onto his rough woollen jumper.

He grinned. "You promised you'd let me paint you, so can we do that today?"

Panic constricted Astrid's throat, but she reluctantly nodded. She had promised.

"Awesome. I thought we could do it in the library, because it has that gorgeous warm light, and the fire will take the chill off. Is that all right?"

Astrid shrugged. "If you want to. But is this dress all right, or do you want me to change into something else?"

"No, you look perfect just the way you are."

Rolling her eyes, yet secretly thrilled by the compliment, she refilled their coffee cups. "Flatterer."

"It's not flattery if it's true though, right?"

Pleasure warmed her, but she tried to tamp it back down. Of course he was being nice to her, he was a guest in her mother's castle – he could hardly insult the daughter of the Queen or treat her poorly.

"Come on."

Clutching her mug as though it would ward off her fear, she followed him into the draughty hallway and headed for the stairs, shivering as an icy blast of wind rattled through a window where the shutters had come loose. Finn caught them just before they crashed against the wall, and after a brief struggle, managed to hook them closed. Then he took Astrid's hand and hurried her into the library. They both sighed with pleasure when they finally stood in front of the crackling fire, and stretched their hands towards the blaze.

"There's something so magical about an open hearth," Finn said, kneeling down to place another log in the heart of it, and smiling as the embers sparked small tongues of flame along the new wood. "Warmth and comfort, for sure, but there's something transformative about it too, that sparks creativity and inflames passion."

He paused, and Astrid wasn't sure whether he was blushing or it was just the heat of the fire turning his cheeks scarlet. She wanted to believe it was passion for her that made him duck his head to hide his burning face, but the rejection by the villagers still stung too much for hope.

Sinking to the floor, she settled her skirts around her and stared into the flames.

"Oh, that's perfect! Don't move a muscle!" Finn exclaimed, and ran out of the room.

Bemused, Astrid stayed where she was and allowed her mind to drift off into dreams of a Christmas with Finn at their table. The festive season had always been fraught, with just her and her mother. There was something sad about the celebration that the Queen refused to speak of, and vague flashes of fights between them whispered in Astrid's mind, although she couldn't remember what they'd fought over. There was a haze around the day, as though her memory had been altered. *Had it?* An image of Finn's eyes clouding over with confusion before he drank the coffee that morning blazed into her mind, and she shuddered.

Was her mother somehow messing with his head as well as hers? Or with everyone's? Is that why Kristina didn't remember staying the night in her chamber? Was the Queen dosing them all with coffee for compliance? And if she could do that, was she controlling the seasons too? Keeping them all in an eternal winter and ensuring Christmas Day never arrived, because it reminded her too painfully of anger and loss?

A hysterical laugh lodged in Astrid's throat, and she clamped her mouth shut to keep it inside. She was being ridiculous, trying to find conspiracies everywhere.

Relief washed over her when her guest rushed back into the room, canvas and easel tucked precariously under one arm, box of paints and brushes in the other hand. "Oh good, you're still in position," he grinned, setting himself up between the window and the fire, so he had good light but didn't freeze to death. "Don't move a muscle!"

As he painted they talked, and the hours stretched out, golden and glorious, both of them lulled by the cosy heat of the room and the intimacy created by the raging storm outside. It was like nothing and no one else in the world existed, and Astrid felt her heart opening, and mending, and filling with tentative hope. The way he gazed at her – so intense, as though he was peering deep into her soul – unsettled her at first, but not in a bad way. She soon became a little more comfortable, and after the first hour she began to find it intoxicating, all of his focus directed at her, and passion and warmth blazing in his eyes.

Cook brought them lunch, and they paused to eat the hearty stew and just-out-of-the-oven bread, then freshly baked scones that practically melted in their mouths. Once their bellies were full, Astrid resumed her position by the fire and Finn returned to the easel. She drifted in daydreams of blue skies and warm sunshine, which all felt more possible as she basked in his close proximity, breathing in his strength and resolve.

Finally he stepped back, gazed at his canvas, and smiled. "It's done! Do you want to come and see?"

Astrid scrunched her face in thought. "Um, maybe?" What if she looked awful? Or worse, what if he'd done a terrible job – what would she say to him?

"Come on, be brave." He walked over and reached a hand down to help her up. "You can tell me what you really think, I won't bite." A shudder snaked up her spine, that he seemed to read her mind again, but she hesitantly approached the easel, then peered around to have a look. And sucked in a gasp of surprise.

"You hate it." Finn sighed. "It's okay. Gran said criticism is the best way to grow and learn and get better, so tell me what's terrible about it. It will be a learning experience."

Astrid was still staring at the painting, transfixed. "It's incredible. You're amazing."

"I'm confused. You look stunned, in a bad way."

Peeking bashfully through the curtain of her hair, she tried to smile. "It's beautiful."

"I don't understand," Finn said, exasperated. "What's wrong with that?"

"Well, you've made me look beautiful," she whispered.

"You are beautiful," he said sternly. "I just painted what is there."

Astrid shook her head. He must be trying to flatter her, or maybe he wanted something from her. Tears threatened, and desperately she wished she was back in her chamber, alone, and never having met this sweet boy who made her feel all these strange new emotions.

"That's not me," she muttered, and wandered away from him, back to the fire, trying to compose herself. Could he really think she looked like the girl in the portrait, the beautiful, kind-hearted, confident woman he'd depicted? More than anything she prayed she was like that, but –

She sensed him moving towards her. All she wanted to do was turn around and throw herself into his arms, yet that would only cause more pain, more rejection.

"We should get ready for dinner. Can't keep Mother waiting," she said quickly, and hurried from the room.

Chapter 10

Kristina was humming a song under her breath as she helped Astrid into a long burgundy dress with a boned bodice, layers of swirling skirts, and touches of lace at the wrists and neckline. The Queen had announced that dinners on Saturday nights would be formal, with Astrid and Finn expected to dress "appropriately".

"You sound happy tonight," Astrid said, sitting down at her dressing table and gazing at her maid in the mirror.

Picking up a brush, Kristina began sweeping it through Astrid's long pale hair. She smiled shyly. "It's nice that you have a reason to dress up, my lady, and someone to talk to. It must be lonely for you usually, stuck here in the castle all on your own," she replied.

Then her hands flew to her mouth as though to take back her words, or at least stifle her gasp of horror. "Oh no! I'm so sorry, my lady, to presume! I didn't mean it!"

"It's okay Kristina. I am often lonely," Astrid admitted, voice cracking with pain. "What was the song you were singing?"

Her maid sighed wistfully, eyes downcast. "It's one Ma sings to my brothers and sisters. It reminds me of when I lived at home with them."

Astrid stared at her, suddenly realising she had no idea who Kristina's family was, or where she was from. She'd never even thought to ask. Did she ever get to go home?

Swallowing nervously, she bit her bottom lip. "Um, where do they live?" she finally ventured. "And how often do you see them?"

"The Queen allows me to visit once a month," Kristina said carefully. "For a day."

Shocked, Astrid swung around and grasped her maid's hand, forcing her to hold her gaze. "What? Why? Where are they? How long does it take to get there?"

"I'm from the village at the bottom of the mountain. Cook said the Queen prefers staff whose families live further away. It takes four hours to walk down, and longer to climb back up, but sometimes I can get a lift with the farrier on his cart, if it's his day to see the horses."

Mind whirring, Astrid tried to make sense of this, but gave up in favour of coming up with some way to improve things. "I'm truly sorry Kristina," she blurted out. "About the situation, and about how oblivious I've been. But from now on you should go home once a week, for at least a day, or two when you can."

She brushed off her maid's protests. "Mother isn't even here mid-week, and you know how infrequently I need help getting dressed in something fancy." She waved wildly at her current outfit, which was a definite aberration. Usually it didn't matter if she got out of bed, or changed out of her nightgown, let alone slipped into something formal. "I beg you, please go and see your family more often. And take my horse, so you get more than a few hours there. I rarely ride her."

"I don't know what to say, my lady," Kristina whispered, eyes wide with hope, and fear.

The poor girl didn't believe she meant it. Astrid reached up and wiped a tear from her maid's eye. "Say: 'I graciously forgive you for being so self-centred all this time, and gladly accept your offer. I will ride your horse down the mountain every Wednesday to see my family.'"

Eyes blurring with unshed tears, her maid nodded. "Thank you," she whispered hoarsely.

"Now, I should get downstairs before I *really* make Mother angry." And pulling her hair into a loose ponytail, Astrid grinned at Kristina and hurried out the door.

Cook had outdone herself with a winter feast fit for, well, a queen, and Astrid wondered what her story was. Did she have family at the castle, or was she like Kristina, only allowed to see her loved ones once a month? Did she have a husband? A *child*? And how had she not considered this before? Maybe the villagers were right. She was a monster. Selfish and self-absorbed, believing herself entitled to whatever and whoever she wanted, no matter the cost to everyone else.

"What are you thinking?" Finn asked, and she forced her attention back to the present, taking in how good he looked in a dark green velvet jacket over a crisp white shirt and black pants. More luxurious handmade clothes that fit him perfectly. What was her mother playing at?

Speak of the devil.

The Queen swept into the room before Astrid could arrange her wild musings into any semblance of order, so she just smiled at Finn and shrugged, relieved to be off the hook for the moment. But she was determined to talk to him about it. She needed to hear the truth. Was she the most selfish and arrogant person in the kingdom?

A few days later, after her mother had stormed away in a swirl of white fur, snowflakes and criticism, Astrid was in the library with Finn, she studying, he researching for his mysterious project. The fire crackled, heating the room and making their cheeks flush red. Astrid's skin crawled as she realised the castle was always a few degrees warmer when the Queen wasn't there. What did her mother do when she was away? Why was she absent so often? And what would be expected of her one day, as the Snow Queen's daughter?

As though sensing her thoughts, Finn glanced up from the book he was reading – *The Politics and Intricacies of Monarchy* – and stared hard at her.

"So, I guess you're officially a princess?"

She shrugged uncomfortably.

"But I haven't heard anyone call you that."

"You haven't heard anyone call me anything, have you?" she said flatly. "Sometimes I feel like I don't even exist. Or if I do, there's no point to it, no point to me."

Wincing, Finn's eyes softened. "I think there's a point to you," he said softly. "I love talking to you, and I'm so grateful that you've made time to hang out with me."

Astrid shrugged. Poor guy, to think *that* was worth anything at all. "What does it say in your book?" she asked, keen to change the subject. "Does it explain what my mother actually does? What I'll be expected to do one day? Do you have a king and queen where you're from?"

Kristina came in, carrying a tray with two steaming mugs of cinnamon-sprinkled hot chocolate, and Finn moved to sit with Astrid on the couch. The sweet scent swirled around them, and his nearness relaxed her mind, while putting her body on high alert.

"We do have a princess near us, although I don't know much about her. I think men have been dying to impress her and win her hand, but she doesn't suffer fools, so she may be alone for a while longer," he said with a chuckle.

Then he turned serious. "But your mother has been ruling alone for a long time, and is respected throughout all the surrounding kingdoms. Closer to home she listens to disputes and decides the outcome, and apparently she's always scrupulously fair. Monarchs also look after their kingdom's defences, although there's been no war here for decades. I guess she'd make sure everyone is fed and clothed, that there are schools and medical assistance. Why, what did you think she did?"

Astrid blushed scarlet. She couldn't tell him she'd long wondered if her mother was causing environmental disaster across the continent – sending more rain to a region in flood, creating avalanches and snow drifts to bury people, or entire towns, in the mountains.

"I don't know," she mumbled. Yet something about his words didn't ring true. "But Cook told Kristina we're running low on food, and she's worried that we'll run out."

Taking a sip of his hot chocolate, then holding it up in front of her, Finn laughed. "It doesn't look like there's a food shortage here, judging by our excellent breakfasts, and amazing dinners, not to mention all the food and drink at the ball the other night. Speaking of which, there's another one this Friday night, right?"

Astrid nodded helplessly. *And the one after that, and the one after that.*

"Do we have to dress up again?"

"We sure do," she replied glumly. "So I'd better go and see Mother's wardrobe mistress to have a new gown made – can't let the family name down."

Sighing, she managed a small smile. "I guess you should come too."

Chapter 11

Their second ball together was as full of pomp and pageantry as the first, but this time Astrid felt a little more confident in her pretty blue gown and sparkling shoes. She interacted more warmly with the guests, greeting them and asking how they were, and when Finn went to get drinks, or a dance required everyone to switch partners, she managed to make small talk with those around her. She loved that everything looked so enchanting, and so welcoming, under the golden glow of the many candelabra.

But the best part was her growing friendship with Finn. She felt more comfortable with him tonight, more able to ask questions and hold her own as they chatted – and less defensive when he asked things of her. They'd met outside the library again so they could walk into the ballroom together, and tonight she didn't hesitate to take his hand and lead him onto the dance floor as soon as the orchestra began playing a waltz.

She didn't even feel as overshadowed by her mother this time, or as painfully aware at every moment of exactly where she was and what she was doing. And she'd swear that one time when she'd caught her eye, her mother had smiled approvingly at her. Wonders would never cease!

Finn seemed more self-assured too, still full of astonishment at the spectacle around them, but not quite as wide-eyed and disbelieving as the week before.

"This is so wonderful Astrid," he announced, as they paused in the dancing to feast on the delicate canapés being passed around on silver platters. "I'm so glad I took your mother up on her offer to come here to do my research. I had no idea it would be so much fun – and no idea that you would be here. That you would be so kind, and so lovely."

She glowed at the compliment, even though she struggled to believe it. And when the clock began chiming midnight, and everyone stared up at the Queen in anticipation, it didn't alarm her that the date flipped backwards from the 23rd to the 17th again, and another solstice ball was announced for the coming Friday. She was growing to like the idea that she could do the night over every week, improving her manner, and her confidence. Becoming more charming, more witty, more dazzling. Maybe over time she would grow into the kind of person Finn could love. Someone with the presence and elegance of her mother, but kinder and sweeter.

She could dream.

"So, it's your turn to paint me now."

"But I can't paint!" Astrid protested, as she poured a waterfall of maple syrup on her pancakes.

Finn laughed, but his gaze was stern. "Of course you can. I've seen your artworks, they're incredible. You can paint anything, and really beautifully too. Come on, what else are we going to do in this storm?"

Fair point. It was the morning after their second ball together, and they'd planned to go out and explore, maybe even ice-skate, but the blizzard still raged, and it didn't look like it would ease any time soon.

"Fine," she muttered grudgingly, then barely spoke as they finished breakfast, too nervous about picking up a brush again and being judged by Finn. Intellectually she knew she used to be able to paint – she'd seen the proof when she showed him the art room – but she couldn't remember doing it. Couldn't remember *how* to do it.

It was one more part of her life that was shrouded in a haze of forgetting, and it worried her that so much was like this. It was all just half remembered wisps of feelings and events, interspersed with glaring gaps. Was she as selfish as the villagers had implied? As self-important and cruelly ignorant as she'd felt when talking to Kristina?

And why couldn't she remember her life? The word "curse" flickered into her mind, but she tried to laugh it off. There may be something weird happening with time, but curses? That seemed a step too far. Still, she found herself giggling at the thought of poor Rapunzel, locked up in her tower for all those years of isolation. She'd certainly felt that sentiment for so much of her life.

But there was someone here with her now, and she should make the most of their time together. Gathering her resolve, she marched up to the art room, Finn trailing in her wake with a huge grin on his face. And once she was standing in front of a blank canvas with a brush in her hand, the techniques all came back to her. "I missed this," she admitted, surprised, as she mixed up more pigment.

"I'm not sure how I could miss something I didn't remember, but this feels... Well, it feels really good. Thank you."

Finn laughed, a smug glint in his eye. "You're very welcome." Then his forehead furrowed.

"What's wrong?" Astrid asked.

Pain flickered across his face. "I don't know, sorry. It's just... I hadn't painted for a long time either, and I can't remember why not." His eyes had that faraway expression again, and Astrid's heart ached for him. For both of them. Who were they, if they didn't remember such crucial things? And yet, did that mean they could reinvent themselves anew?

Maybe it was a good thing that she couldn't remember her old self, if she'd been as arrogant and self-centred as she feared. Perhaps this was a blessing, not a curse, and she could start over with a clean slate, and be kind, and considerate. Listen to people, ask them about themselves, and what she could do to help them.

Maybe she should go down the mountain with Kristina when she visited her family, and take them some food. Perhaps she could gift Emilja and her siblings warm jackets and scarves. Show them that she cared about more than just herself. Prove she wanted to change, and would change.

"So, where would you like me to sit?" Finn broke into her thoughts, and she turned her attention back to him.

"Over there, by the window."

Once she started painting, she barely spoke again, hardly even glanced at her friend. When he asked if she was hungry, she looked over at him in surprise. Half the day had passed, and she'd been oblivious. "I'm fine, but you grab something. I don't want to stop."

"But won't it be hard to keep going if I'm not here to be the model?"

She shook her head. She wasn't painting him sitting in the room with her, she was painting him from her head, or her heart. Some image she hadn't physically seen, but which was pouring out of her onto the canvas.

Shrugging, Finn left the room, and Astrid painted on, her brush strokes becoming faster, more urgent, the image taking shape until she could almost reach out and touch the petals of the flowers in the foreground.

When Finn tapped her on the shoulder an hour later, she jumped, startled, but was grateful for the sandwich he handed her. Now she thought about it, she was kind of hungry.

She bit into the sandwich and swallowed quickly, then put down the plate, her hands shaking too much to hold it.

"Thank you," she mumbled, wiping crumbs from her mouth. "Um, I think I'm done. But please don't be too harsh. It's my first attempt in... I don't know how long."

Stepping away from the easel, she took another bite of the sandwich and tried to steel herself for his assessment. Then she noticed Finn's face.

"What's wrong?" she asked shrilly, filled with panic and fear. "Is it really that bad?"

She'd painted him in front of a small white cottage with a thatched roof, and sunflowers growing in the front garden. Ivy wound its way around the door frame, and through the front window you could see a white candle burning on a wooden table, its warm golden glow illuminating the vase of deep red roses that stood next to it, with a ladybird curled up on one of the petals. Pale lacy curtains looked as though they were moving in a gentle breeze, and there was a handmade woollen blanket in various shades of purple folded over the back of a chair.

The cottage next to it leaned in slightly towards it, as though whispering a secret to its neighbour.

"What is this?" Finn demanded angrily.

Astrid tensed, and stared at him in bewilderment. "What do you mean?"

"How could you know what my house looks like, when I had forgotten?"

Crossing her arms defensively, she watched as he peered more closely at the painting. "But I didn't know," she whispered, perplexed.

"That blanket, my grandma knitted it, although she still had a last section of it to finish before I... left." He paused, distressed, and Astrid moved forward, wanting to comfort him. Reaching out a hand, she touched his shoulder, but he shrugged her off and leaned in closer to the canvas.

"And the roses..." His breath caught. "Greta brought us the roses, from her own garden." His eyes flickered to the second cottage, and Astrid noticed the shadow of a girl's form in the front window, peering out at them with a suspicious look on her face.

"Who's Greta?"

His lips trembled, and Astrid's heart ached.

"I miss her so much," Finn said softly, achingly. Then he ran out of the room.

Chapter 12

Finn didn't come down for dinner that night, or breakfast the following morning, and Astrid could only shrug helplessly when her mother grilled her on where he was.

"Oh Astrid, I've handed him to you on a platter, what more do you want of me?" the Queen asked, condescension dripping from each word. "Still, perhaps it's a good thing you don't spend every minute together, because we don't want him getting sick of you. And you should be studying, and him working. But I must say, that portrait he did of you is wonderful. He made you look beautiful."

The surprise in her voice stung Astrid, yet didn't surprise her. She wondered if her mother knew that she painted too. Yet she couldn't remember her ever encouraging anything she did, or wanted to do, so maybe it was for the best that she didn't enlighten her. The Queen would only berate her daughter for one more apparent failure.

Her heart hurt though, knowing she'd upset her friend. She was desperate to ask Finn what she'd done wrong, so she could try to make amends, and assure him that she'd never do it again. As soon as her mother stormed off to work, she went back up to the art room and peered at the painting. Somehow she'd dreamed Finn's actual home onto the canvas, although she had no idea how. And she'd reminded him of the grandmother who'd raised him, the one he'd told her about in the library when he first arrived, but hadn't mentioned again. How could he have forgotten her?

More importantly than that though was the girl in the other cottage. Who was she? And what was she to Finn? Leaning forward, she narrowed her eyes and tried to make out her features, but she was just a swirl of mist and shadow. Was she Finn's beloved? Did she have his heart? And did she know where he was, off on this visit to the frozen kingdom, or was she waiting at home, worrying about him, wondering if he'd ever return?

A sharp, unfamiliar pang of jealousy stabbed at her, and her breathing grew shallow. One part of her felt for this mysterious girl, but the other part, the bigger part, wanted to make Finn forget her. Gently lifting the canvas from the easel, she placed it at the back of a large rack of paintings. She didn't want to destroy it, because if he left her, she'd need something to remember him by, but she couldn't have him seeing it every day and remembering that Astrid had hurt him – or how much he missed the girl in the picture.

Pacing around the studio, she tried to make sense of everything. There were things she couldn't remember, and it seemed Finn was losing his recall too, at least of the things that were important to him. Had her mother cast a spell of forgetting on her and the villagers, that Finn had somehow become entangled in? And if so, how did it work? She was desperate to understand it, but not so she could give Finn back his memories. Her face flushed with shame. She wanted to make sure the spell continued, so Greta remained far from his mind, and Astrid was secure in his companionship. She wanted him to stay here with her, and let go of his ties to his family and friends. To his grandmother, but mostly to Greta.

Rattled by the selfishness of her desire, she stared out the window, mesmerised by the snow, and focusing on the patterns of the flakes as they fell. There seemed to be a pattern to what was veiled from her, and from Finn, as though the more important it was, the further it fell from the mind.

Was that the secret? The things that meant the most to a person were the ones that couldn't be recalled? She'd forgotten her beautiful friendship with Emilja, as well as the horror of what she'd done to her. So if she avoided reminding Finn of the life he had back home, would the specifics of his loved ones fall away again? What were the most wonderful and most terrible parts of his life? Perhaps if she discovered that, she could ensure he never left her.

She smiled, then felt a sharp twinge of guilt. But she pushed it down, because surely it was best for Finn too, to stay here and live in the luxury of the castle, free to pursue his art, which, after all, was the thing he'd said he wanted most in the whole world.

Trying to convince herself her intentions were pure, she decided to do something worthy. Emilja and her family, and probably most of the villagers, must need thick coats and blankets to endure the eternal winter. Hurrying back downstairs, she sought out the castle steward.

He looked surprised, but pleased, when she burst into his office. "My lady, good morning, how may I help you?"

Then his voice hitched in his throat, and his face paled. "Is everything all right?"

"Yes, thank you," she said, trying to temper her impatience. "The kids who came the other night, they must need warm clothes and blankets, and... I don't know, food? And fuel probably, or something..." Her voice trailed off. How embarrassing. He must think she was a fool, rambling incoherently about people who had been mean to her.

But he didn't. He looked... *proud*... of her?

"That's very kind of you, my lady. And I can organise that for you. Would you like to accompany me down to the village, or should I go on your behalf?"

She wanted to tell him to go alone – she was terrified of seeing Emilja, Vika, Jonas or Kye again – but if she wanted to be a better person, and prove to them that she was, she had to go down there and face them. Prove she could forgive their nasty outbursts, and offer help when it was needed.

"I'll come with you," she said reluctantly.

"As you wish. I'll organise everything now, and meet you at the front of the castle in two hours. Would that suit you, my lady?"

Nodding quickly, she turned on her heel and hurried away, before she could chicken out and tell him to forget it. Back in her chamber, she rummaged through her closet, pulling out all but three warm, waterproof coats, and all but three pairs of fur-lined boots. She sighed. She really did have a lot of clothes, and some of them she'd never even worn. She cringed. No wonder everyone thought she was stuck up and entitled.

Turning her attention to her drawers, she found her favourite three pairs of gloves, threw them onto her bed, then placed the remaining ones in a large washing bag. She repeated the process with dresses, warm and practical trousers and tops, scarves, and even flannel nightgowns, until she'd filled three bags to overflowing, and slimmed down her own possessions significantly. She was surprised how light it made her feel, as though a weight had been lifted from her shoulders.

Kristina came in just as she was trying to drag the bags across the chamber to the door.

"My lady, what on earth are you doing?" her maid demanded, alarmed. "You only have to ask me and I'll do anything laborious, you know that."

Giggling, Astrid dropped the bags and collapsed onto a chair. "Thank you Kristina, I'm embarrassed to admit that I do need some help."

"But what's it for?"

She blushed, suddenly unsure of what she was doing. Would Kristina be offended by her attempts at charity? Find it patronising, or the wrong kind of help? "I'm organising some clothes and blankets for the villagers. The castle steward is helping me," she blurted out.

Kristina looked surprised, then hurt.

It took a moment for Astrid to figure out why, then she sprang into action. "And I thought we could take half of what we've collected down to your village on Wednesday, if that would be useful, or wanted?" she asked quickly. Then she leapt to her feet and hurried to her wardrobe. She'd only kept three long winter coats for herself, but her maid needed one more urgently than she required multiple style options.

"And I thought that you might like this one?" she offered softly.

Tears filled her maid's incredulous eyes. "Really?"

"Please," Astrid said, remembering how cold the girl had been the night she'd stayed in her chamber with her. She'd told her she had no coat, but it had taken until now for the message to get through Astrid's thick skull.

Kristina snatched the coat, as though scared Astrid would change her mind, and gently stroked the woollen fabric. "But what about the Queen, if she sees me wearing this? Will I get into trouble? Will you?"

"She won't even notice," Astrid assured her. How sad that the woman who was supposed to look after the kingdom and its people didn't know how her staff lived, or notice how cold and hungry they were as they waited on her hand and foot. That she wouldn't look at them closely enough to see one of them was wearing her daughter's clothes. "Could I go with you to your village on Wednesday to deliver them? We can take the horse and cart."

Squealing with excitement, Kristina nodded, rushed over and hugged Astrid, then fled the chamber, the coat held tightly and possessively in her arms.

Astrid divided the three large bags into six smaller ones, and picked up three for today's distribution. When she returned to the castle steward's office, she was stunned to see the many piles of blankets, quilts, clothes and boots that he'd managed to rustle up, and he seemed equally impressed by her contributions.

"I think we should keep half of everything though, and take it down to Kristina's village on Wednesday, if that's okay?" she asked him. "Her family lives at the bottom of the mountain. Would you be able to help me?"

"I would be honoured."

Chapter 13

It had surprised Astrid how good it felt to help others. On Monday she and the castle steward had driven the carriage down to the local village, and gone from door to door distributing the blankets, clothes and supplies they'd wrangled together. Emilja was at school, which was mostly a relief – as much as Astrid longed to see her again, the greater part of her had been terrified to face her. One of her younger sisters smiled up at Astrid though, and dipped a deep curtsey before thanking her in a trembling voice, then quickly hiding behind her mother.

"We appreciate it greatly, my lady," the girl's mother said, but Astrid didn't miss the suspicion in her eyes, the hooded glare at the castle steward, or the speed with which she shut the door to their cottage. The cottage Astrid had once stayed in, experiencing the joy of a huge and loving family for the first time.

She supposed it would take a long time to win over the villagers and prove that she wasn't the selfish, stuck-up princess they imagined.

That she'd been.

Her Wednesday visit to the village at the bottom of the mountain took much longer, but was even more successful. Kristina's family were delighted to see her again so soon, and rushed forward to hug her and drag her inside. Astrid and the castle steward left them laughing and talking over each other, then spent the day walking through the narrow, snow-blanketed streets, handing out supplies, and asking the occupants their concerns. It broke Astrid's heart to see that they were all so thin and frail, so bent-shouldered by work, and so sallow-skinned from the endless winter.

She was grateful to the steward for his support – for lifting her with a gentle but firm hand under her elbow whenever she thought she would stumble, for explaining their purpose when she couldn't find her voice, and for distributing what they'd brought so fairly and evenly throughout the small village.

"Thank you," she said softly, when the sun was starting to sink in the west, and they were making their way back to meet Kristina so they could all return to the castle.

"Thank *you*," he responded, offering his arm as the sky darkened and the narrow cobblestone path grew harder to see. "I'm so proud of you Astrid... I mean, my lady. You did something wonderful today, and I know how grateful Kristina is that you're allowing her to see her family more often. You've done a beautiful thing."

Shrugging as she awkwardly pulled herself back up into the now-empty carriage, Astrid muttered that it was only fair a girl could see her mother regularly, then lapsed into silence. She knew she shouldn't be jealous of her maid, who had so little, but her heart had ached when she watched Kristina greet her family. Swinging a new babe up on her hip, wiping a smudge of dirt from a young sister's cheek, asking a small brother where his favourite toy was, hugging another boy with the arm that wasn't clutching the baby. Then laughing with such joyful abandon and throwing herself into her mother's arms when they caught sight of each other.

The woman had looked appraisingly at Astrid, and she'd felt stripped bare, exposed to a tumult of emotion sparked by her knowing gaze. Tears had threatened, and weakness risen within her, but then the woman had dipped her head and mouthed "thank you", before pulling her daughter into the tiny, packed home that spilled laughter and candlelight out onto the dirty laneway.

Gazing out the carriage window now at the stars strewn like diamonds across the velvet twilight sky, Astrid wondered whether she would swap her life in the castle for a tiny cottage, drudgery, and friends and family who loved her, and decided she probably would.

Alone again, Astrid was moping over her breakfast the next morning when Finn came in, looking sheepish, and sat down opposite her.

"I'm really sorry Astrid," he said quickly. "I was a selfish brat the other day, self-absorbed and cruel, and behaved terribly towards you. Can you forgive me? I tried to find you yesterday to apologise, and make amends, but no one knew where you were. I couldn't even find Kristina." He frowned. "I hope you're all right?"

Astrid smiled, her heart lifting and her mood suddenly sunny despite the grey light creeping faintly into the room. "I'm fine." She'd been looking forward to impressing him with the good deeds she'd performed, and opened her mouth to detail what she'd done and how people had responded to her. But before she could begin, the Queen swept in and took her place at the head of the table. First she berated the serving girl, complaining about the absence of coffee, then she turned to Finn and engaged him in a conversation about the politics of his region.

Astrid held her breath, worried that talking about his home would stir up more of his memories – and return Greta to the front of his mind. But he spoke of his village, and the wider region, without faltering, keeping his comments light and impersonal, restricted to how the council there worked, and how its running could be improved. Astrid was impressed.

So was the Queen, who beamed at him. "And do you plan to return there? To take a seat on their council?"

Finn laughed. "Goodness no. Although we have elections, they don't really have any bearing on the results – our council positions pretty much just get handed down father to son. I can't think of a single person who was elected from amongst us commoners, or a single woman, if I think about it."

Confusion shadowed his eyes, and his brow furrowed as he gazed at the Queen's silver tiara. It was more subtle than the ones she wore to the balls, but the power that emanated from it could still be felt. No one would challenge her right to rule, or her capability to do the job. Why would a local council deny women the right to be involved and make a contribution? And why had the absence of women never registered in his mind?

"Well, you'll make a wonderful leader one day Finn," the Queen said, then turned to her daughter, face hard. "You should use the time you have to learn from Finn, because his depth of knowledge in so many areas is outstanding, unlike yours."

Muttering under her breath while managing to smile and nod politely, Astrid caught Finn's eye, then tried to smother her laugh. He was frowning in consternation at her mother, clearly not impressed by her words – and thankfully still in the present moment, not pining for anyone back home. She knew it was cruel to want him to forget those closest to him, but she needed him more than they did. Although impinging on his free will made her far more similar to her mother than she was comfortable with, and she squirmed in her seat.

"With all due respect, Your Majesty, you're selling your daughter very short," Finn said, shocking Astrid with his impertinence as well as his words. "She is clever and kind, well-read and full of consideration and empathy, and she will make a wise ruler when her time comes."

Astrid glowed at his praise, then turned nervously to her mother. The Queen didn't like being challenged, and people had been severely punished for far less, yet she was smiling at Finn. It was a smug smile, granted, but the anger and condescension she'd expected just wasn't there.

How strange. Her mother couldn't really want her and Finn to fall for each other, could she?

Why would she do that?

Finally the Queen departed, leaving them to their own devices until the ball the following night. After more apologies from Finn for the painting fiasco, which Astrid graciously accepted, they reverted to their former friendship, working side by side in the library during daylight hours, then sitting together in the evening drinking hot chocolate by the fire and discussing books, politics, history and philosophy.

Finn had been impressed by her generous offer to Kristina, and her determination to make it happen right away, as well as her visit to the mountain villages. "You're not just all talk, like so many people," he said. "I'm proud of you Astrid, for stepping up when you saw a need, even in the face of your mother's derision."

She smiled wistfully. "You make me want to be a better person Finn. I'm ashamed to admit that it hadn't really occurred to me to wonder about them before, or do anything to help. I was so wrapped up in my own loneliness and my own pathetic problems – which pale to nothing compared to their efforts just to survive, to keep their children fed and warm. It's been really good for me to have you here, pushing me, challenging me, and forcing me out of my pathetic pity party."

Finn reached over and took her hand, and her stomach flipped, butterflies dancing as her pulse quickened. "Don't do that," he said softly. "Don't sell yourself short, the way your mother does. She's wrong about you, and that's a fault in her, not you. You are kind and compassionate, and have a very caring heart. You'll make a great ruler one day, truly."

A blush stained her cheeks, and she let her pale hair tumble down over her shoulders, hiding her face while she shook her head. "That won't happen."

"And when it does?"

She shrugged. "I don't want to rule. I'm not capable, or qualified. And I don't think Mother has any plans for letting me take over either, which is fine." She winced as she remembered the anger and derision on the faces of her former classmates at the ball. The scorn and hatred in Emilja's voice.

"No one likes me, and I don't have what it takes to be a queen. I don't even know what Mother does, where she goes when she's supposedly working, or what the job entails. And to be brutally honest, I don't think we're needed. People would get on just as well without us. Maybe better." The gaunt faces of the villagers sprang to her mind, contrasted with the bright-eyed dancers at the balls. She'd never noticed the discrepancy between the lords and ladies of the aristocracy, who lived in rich halls on the nearby mountains, and the poverty and injustice of the people who barely eked out a living providing labour for their so-called superiors.

"The people who come to the solstice balls love your mother, and are grateful to be in her presence," Finn protested. "And I've seen the way they look at you too, with admiration and respect. You don't notice it, because you're too shy to catch their eye, but I promise you, they will be very happy when the time comes for you to fill the Queen's shoes."

Astrid trembled at the thought, and quickly changed the subject. But when she finally went to bed, sleep eluded her altogether as her heart raced and her imagination ran wild. She'd never seriously considered ruling the people of this snowbound kingdom, had never dared to believe she was capable of it. But Finn's faith in her, and his gentle encouragement, were making her feel it could be possible. And it would be even easier if Finn stayed here and ruled with her. Was that her mother's plan?

Cautiously she began to envision herself accepting the responsibility, embracing it even. What should she be doing to prepare? Had she been tutored in politics and governance but forgotten it, or was her mother waiting for her to show an interest before those lessons began? Testing her out for her suitability? Had she lured Finn to the castle hoping he would be a good influence on her daughter, and spark her interest in studying to be a ruler?

On the verge of finally being dragged into slumber, Astrid giggled. She was certainly interested in studying Finn, and dreaming of potential futures with him, crown or no crown.

Chapter 14

A few nights later the clouds momentarily parted, and Astrid grabbed the thickest coats she could find, and a flask full of hot chocolate, and bundled Finn up the narrow spiral staircase to the roof. They sat together out in the frosty evening air, sprawled on a thick blanket and gazing up at the beauty of the star-strewn sky overhead, and the swirling colours of the northern lights as they danced across the heavens.

A puff of breath misted around them as Finn leaned back on his elbows and sighed.

Panic gripped Astrid. "What's wrong?" she asked nervously, wanting to soothe his hurt, but terrified he'd somehow been reminded of his old life. That he was sick of her, and wanted to leave her and return home.

"Nothing's wrong," he said quickly. "Everything finally feels right. It's like I can see again. See how much beauty there is in the world, how much potential. For a while it was as though I was peering at the world through the devil's mirror, vision obscured, and finding fault in everything. I was seeing darkness in light, ugliness in beauty, weakness in kind-heartedness. I wasn't myself, wasn't as caring as I usually am, but I didn't know how to stop it. How to be myself again."

He shivered, then wrapped his arms around himself, trying to self-soothe, and looking so sad and filled with regret that Astrid's heart ached for him. "I was so cold all the time, so stiff, so divorced from my emotions," he continued. "I was going through the motions – school, work, sleep, repeat – but I wasn't really there."

Pausing for a moment, he smiled ruefully at Astrid as he took the mug of hot chocolate she offered him, wrapping his fingers tightly around it and blowing on the steaming surface before taking a cautious sip.

"I'm sorry," Astrid whispered, not wanting to interrupt, but needing him to know she was there for him.

"You don't have to apologise! On the contrary, you're the one who's helping me the most. I'd stopped seeing the magic in the world. I passed the northern lights on my way here and barely glanced at them, but now I can't drink them in fast enough. Talking to you is opening my eyes again to wonder and awe. Being with you is thawing my frozen heart," he whispered, face moving closer to hers, a small smile lifting the corners of his mouth, and a fire that seemed like a promise burning in his eyes. "You're warming me back up Astrid, and bringing me back to life."

Shocked, she stared up at him. Did this mean he really did like her? Anticipation flooded her body, her tummy tightening and her eyes glued to Finn's full lips, imagining what it would feel like if they met hers. She'd never kissed a boy, but oh, how desperately she wanted to kiss Finn.

"I'm sorry I got weird with you about the painting," he said softly, drawing back slightly to speak.

Astrid felt physical pain at the loss of his closeness, an emptiness already weaving through her.

"It's beautiful, it just brought up so many strange and unfamiliar emotions, none of which I can really articulate. But that's what great art should do," he insisted, passion rising in his voice. "You're really talented Astrid, amazingly talented, and if that's what you want to do with your life, you should definitely pursue it."

"I'm not sure I have the courage," she replied sadly. "And where would I even start? I haven't been to school, I don't know any universities, and I'm not sure Mother would let me leave anyway." She lowered her eyes, crestfallen. "It's funny, before I met you, I didn't feel trapped –"

"What!?" Finn spluttered, looking horrified. "I make you feel trapped?"

Shaking her head, Astrid lay a consoling hand on his arm. "I mean I didn't feel enough of anything before you arrived to even know there was another life out there. Other people, other choices. Now, who knows…"

She trailed off and gazed back up at the stars. "It's all so beautiful. So limitless. And I'm glad I feel differently now. I'm glad you came. It feels like I've woken up from a hundred-year sleep."

Darkness swirled around them, comforting, concealing, drawing them together. It was so intimate, as though not being able to see each other meant they could bare their souls and reveal their deepest secrets.

"I'm glad I came too," Finn said, voice husky. "Because I feel like I've woken up as well. I always loved nature, loved the sky and the planets, but something happened to me before I left home. I didn't just stop seeing the beauty and magic around me, I also lashed out at the people closest to me. Sometimes I get these flashes of me arguing with someone, of slamming doors, of the face of a friend crumpling because I was so cruel. Of feeling so deeply, deeply unhappy."

Finn leaned down and gently stroked her cheek. "But that's gone now."

His voice was a whisper, a caress, and Astrid's heart thundered and her mouth grew dry. Cautiously she leaned into him, drowning in his eyes as the northern lights glittered from within their depths, igniting a fire in her soul and a slow burn along her skin. She shivered as she held his gaze, trying to name the swirl of emotions he was sparking within her, and figure out what it was he felt for her.

She'd never been so listened to, so encouraged, so *seen*. The barriers she'd clung to so tightly no longer felt necessary. Her whole being was slowly unfurling, and yearning to love, despite her doubts and insecurities.

Finn's mouth was almost on hers when a snowflake fell on Astrid's nose, and she giggled. Then cursed under her breath as Finn stiffened and pulled away.

No! How could she have ruined the moment like that? The distance between them now felt like an abyss, impenetrable. As though they hadn't just been leaning in to each other, baring their souls, preparing to take a chance. Had she got it so wrong? Misread his signals? Tears stung her eyes, but she blinked them back, determined not to show any weakness, or reveal any hurt.

But the bone-deep fear that he was relieved she'd broken the spell pierced her heart. Now he looked embarrassed by how close they'd come to kissing, and she burned with humiliation, desperate to flee to her chamber and hide herself away. How could she have imagined that he might be interested in her? He'd praised her painting to be polite, because he was a guest here. He wanted to stay in her mother's good graces. What had possessed her to imagine he could like *her*? To bring him up to the roof on this sweetly scented black-velvet night, alone together in the beautiful dark?

A flurry of snowflakes landed on them, and Astrid dragged herself to her feet, bitterness and regret hollowing her out. She'd been right all along. She'd always known she was destined to be alone. No friends, no family to speak of, and no chance of ever finding love. But it wasn't fair!

"Hey, what happened?" Finn asked, trying to catch up with her as she stalked towards the door back into the castle. "Are you okay?"

"Fine," she muttered. Desperately trying to hold on to her composure, she avoided his eyes, relieved when she reached the top of the stairs and could make her way back down and to the safety of her room.

"Ouch!"

Heart racing in alarm, Astrid swung around and peered anxiously up at Finn. He'd cracked his head on a low beam, and was now rubbing his forehead and muttering curses under his breath.

"Are you all right?"

He smiled wistfully. "I will be. But what about you?" He started to reach for her, but she quickly turned back to the stairs, ducked her head low and hurried down.

Once they reached the corridor and Astrid knew he was okay, she fled to her chamber and buried herself under the bedclothes, mortified that she'd allowed herself to be so vulnerable, and made such a fool of herself.

How would she face Finn again, now that he knew she wanted to kiss him?

She was a bundle of nerves as she staggered down to breakfast the next morning, terrified she'd scared Finn away for good. But when she reluctantly walked in and pulled a chair up to the table, he simply poured her a cup of coffee and smiled as he usually did.

"How did you sleep?"

A flush stained her cheeks pink as she recalled the dream of Finn she'd had, but she managed to stammer: "Pretty good, and you?"

As he waxed lyrical about the comfortable bed and warm fire, she realised he held no grudge, and didn't think any less of her. For a moment she wondered if their awkward almost-kiss had even happened. Until she noticed how fast he was talking, and realised he was anxious too.

Oh god, had he thought she was laughing at *him* when the snowflake landed on her nose? That *she* hadn't wanted to kiss *him*?

Why was everything so complicated?

Distracted, she finished breakfast and followed him to the library, then started on her lessons. For once she actually wanted to dive into them so she could think about something other than Finn, and her tutor seemed surprised yet delighted with her dedication.

When Kristina brought lunch several hours later, they'd both shrugged off any awkwardness, and by the time their fourth ball together came around a few days later, their friendship was close and comfortable again. They spent the whole night in each other's company, dancing for hours, sipping sneakily on glasses of the spiced red wine they stole from the waiters, and dreaming up imagined lives for the strangers who filled the ballroom with their glamorous clothes, dazzling faces and glittering laughter.

Pushing away thoughts of the hungry people in the villages below them, she assuaged her guilt with a vow to take more food to them the next time her mother left the castle. Although Cook was apparently worried about their own supplies, they clearly had enough to feed the local lords and ladies. Or was the price of admission to the Yule ball a share of *their* store cupboards and cellars? How did her mother raise money to keep the kingdom running?

A tug on her hand brought her back to the present, and Finn spun her back out onto the dance floor. Astrid lost herself in the music, the enchantment of the evening, and the magic of being held close in his arms. She had no idea how long he was going to stay, but for tonight she was going to imagine that this could be her life. Reading with him in the library or painting together during the day, and staring up at the stars or dancing cheek to cheek by night. She would dare to dream that she could have someone in her life who really cared about her. Who appreciated what she had to say, and would support and encourage whatever she wanted to do with her future.

Finn seemed just as content to be with her, his wide smile and newfound confidence wearing a suit contributing to the joy bubbling from him. But finally the night wore down, the clock struck midnight, and the Queen stood up and thanked everyone for coming.

"It's always a pleasure to spend time with you," she called out, her voice booming to every corner of the room.

"I hope you enjoyed the mulled wine and other festive treats – and I hope you will all return next Friday night, to celebrate the winter solstice at our special Yule ball."

Cheering broke out around the room, but Finn turned to Astrid in surprise. "What does she mean? I thought tonight was the winter solstice ball." For a moment his eyes looked glazed, and a frown of concentration marred his brow.

Astrid shrugged, unsure how to address his memory loss, especially if it made it easier for him to stay. "I rarely understand anything my mother says, or does. I guess she's just extending the season of goodwill?"

Finn blinked, then smiled. "Cool. Far be it for me to turn down another night dancing with you, my lady!" And he grabbed her hand and spun her around, before leading her out of the ballroom.

Astrid tried to laugh it off, but her heart was racing. Did he know something was wrong too? She felt a trap tightening around her. What did it mean? And how would it end? Surely time couldn't spin in on itself forever.

What would happen when it broke?

Chapter 15

Astrid's voice was as gloomy as her face when she saw Finn the next morning. "I was hoping today would be fine, so we could picnic in the woods, but it feels like the sky will never clear." She sighed dramatically. "I can't even remember the last time I saw the sun."

"Don't pout." Finn lifted her chin and smiled at her. "There's got to be something we can do. What if we lay out a rug in the library and have the picnic there, in front of the fire?"

"Huh. That sounds perfect."

It was Finn's turn to pout. "You don't have to look quite so surprised."

Giggling, Astrid gulped down the rest of her coffee then scraped back her chair and stood up. "Meet you there at midday?"

Finn nodded, ate a final bite of toast, then headed up to the art room, while Astrid skipped down the stairs to the kitchens to sort out a basket of food. Excitement fizzed within her. She didn't want to get her hopes up, but Finn could have gone off on his own all day, or locked himself in the studio and painted until nightfall, but he'd suggested they do something together. Could he be starting to feel for her, the way she did for him? After the heartbreak of the night with the villagers, it soothed her soul to know he wanted to spend time with her. Had *chosen* to.

It felt like the three hours until noon would never pass. Astrid paced impatiently around her room, flicked endlessly through her now-depleted wardrobe in search of inspiration, then stared out her window at the frozen wasteland that stretched away into the distance in a thick, endless blanket of pure, glaring white. She cursed it for trapping her inside and bringing her life to a standstill – yet it was somehow beautiful in its harshness. And she had to admit she was grateful to it too, because the endless winter was keeping Finn here in the castle with her.

When the clock struck twelve and they reconvened in the library, they talked for hours, munching on hot savoury pies and sipping hot chocolate, laughing while they swapped stories and wild theories about guests at past balls, then growing more serious as they discussed books, artists and painting techniques they loved.

Astrid wondered if her parents had ever sat together like this, losing themselves in each other, their conversations weaving around them and pulling them closer, as they shared their dreams and revealed the things that mattered most to them. She'd never known her father, and she ached for the missing piece of herself that his death had left. And she yearned for the mother she'd lost too, the carefree young woman who'd married her Prince Charming and started her rule with such optimism and kindness, or so she'd been told.

She'd never met that woman either, but she was starting to appreciate that her mother's cold, remote demeanour was at least partly a response to her grief, to the desperation and mourning she'd been plunged into as a young wife, pregnant with her first child, who lost everything to a hiking accident in these ragged, ice-covered mountains. Well, she hadn't lost her child, yet she acted that way most of the time, Astrid thought bitterly. As though she wasn't even here. As though she had no daughter.

A gentle hand on her arm brought her tumbling back to the present, and she blinked rapidly to reorientate herself in the room – and try to keep the tears welling in her eyes from failing.

"Are you okay?"

She nodded, and tried to smile at Finn. Tried to calm her beating heart.

Then he plunged a dagger deep into her chest. "Have you met any of the people from the village down the hill? I know how lonely you've been, but surely you'd find some wonderful friends there, people your age?"

Biting her lip to try to keep her groan in, she took a deep breath to steady her wild pulse, anchor her back in this room, and figure out what to say. How could she tell him what had happened without giving away her own cruelty – and her knowledge that her mother was making them forget things?

Mistaking her silence, Finn's voice hardened. "Or is there some castle rule that you're not allowed to associate with the commoners?"

"No! Nothing like that!" she said quickly, defensively. "*They* don't want to associate with me!" The hot shame burned in her belly, and her cheeks flushed.

Finn stared at her, brow furrowed. "I can't believe that."

"It's true," she insisted, voice low and trembling. "The week before you arrived, I went to my first ball. Mother had always said I was too young, but, well, I let her know how lonely I was, so she invited some of the teenagers from the village, and we had a brilliant night, exploring the castle, dancing together, chatting for hours."

"See!"

She plunged onward. "But at the end of the night, it all went horribly wrong."

Her eyes stung, and she scrubbed at them impatiently. "They all turned on me, and were really nasty. They said they couldn't stand me, and never wanted to see me again." Her voice hitched. "Am I really so unlikeable?"

Finn's face softened. "Of course not. You're sweet and kind, and smart and talented, and so much fun to spend time with. Perhaps they're just jealous that you live in the castle, and are projecting on to you. Maybe it's about them, not you."

Now she did start weeping. "That's the sweetest thing anyone has ever said to me," she sobbed.

Finn drew her into his arms and stroked her hair. "Shhh, don't cry lovely Astrid. It's their loss, if they can't see your worth. Besides, speaking selfishly, it's good for me, because I get you all to myself."

"Really?"

He nodded, then lowered his lips close to her ear, and his voice to a whisper. "Cross my heart."

Inhaling sharply, Astrid's pulse quickened at the warmth of his breath on her cheek, and the hairs on her arms stood up, flesh covered in goosebumps. Desperately she tried to pull herself together, to appear calm and composed, but her body betrayed her with a loud hiccup. She groaned inwardly. *Real smooth.*

But Finn just grinned at her embarrassment. "Now, shall we go make some art? I think we should both paint a summer beach scene, and whoever creates the most beautiful one wins."

"You're on."

*A*strid's tears had all dried, and her breathing was under control, by the time she and Finn were ensconced in the art room together. They each set up in front of an easel with a blank canvas, positioned so they could see each other, but not what they were working on. Yet it hardly mattered. She didn't need to compare herself or get intimidated by Finn's skill, or search for inspiration, because while she'd never been to the ocean, never strolled along a sunny shoreline, the moment he'd mentioned the challenge, she'd known exactly what to paint.

Closing her eyes for a moment, she let the scene that played out in her dreams so often, of the two of them walking hand in hand along the golden sands of a tropical beach together, flood her mind and her senses. The dream had started long before she'd met Finn for the first time, and while that had frightened her at first, now she was convinced – or hopeful at least – that it was fate. Or magic. Some kind of beautiful faery tale finally playing out as a reward for surviving her so-far-miserable life.

Mixing the enchanting green shade of his eyes on her palette then glancing up at him, she smiled in wonder. Somehow the universe had conspired to bring them together, and she was determined to make the most of the opportunity. Surely it meant something that they both loved art, craved it, and that they could express themselves in this way – even if they'd both rejected it for a time.

"So, um, didn't you miss painting when you stopped?" she asked cautiously. "You're so talented, and it seems like it's a part of your very soul, an expression of your deepest self. I can't imagine how you could feel whole without it."

A storm of emotions flitted across Finn's face – a quicksilver flash of anger, immediately chased away by a moment of pain, and the hollow look of regret – then a cloud of self-doubt furrowed his brow.

"We don't have to talk about it," Astrid said hurriedly, stomach tightening with worry that she'd upset him, and remorse that she'd brought it up. "I don't mean to pry, I promise."

But he smiled at her, a real smile, and this time it reached his eyes. "We can talk about it," he assured her. "I'm just not sure how to explain it without sounding, I don't know, too strange, or too self-absorbed."

Astrid snorted. "You've seen my life – it would take a lot for me to think any one or any thing is strange. And according to the villagers, no one is more arrogant or up themselves than me."

Finn's face softened. "I was encouraged to draw when I was young, and I did – plants, mountains, river sprites, gnomes, faeries – things from the stories my gran told. I really enjoyed it, and it made me feel good when people loved what I created." A blush stained his cheeks, and he gazed out the window, eyes unfocused, mind wandering as he tried to recall memories both happy and harsh.

Finally he looked back at Astrid. "I was always the youngest in my class, and I felt intimidated by the older boys. About a year ago, they became more interested in girls, in competing with each other, and they started making fun of me for being artistic. Told me I had to grow up, and leave such 'girlie' pursuits to the children."

He winced. "I'm ashamed to admit this, but their mockery affected me. I know I should have just laughed it off, ignored them, kept painting. But I desperately wanted them to like me, to accept me, so I stopped going to the art room after school, and instead spent my afternoons with them." He grimaced, but continued.

"We'd all try to outdo each other in feats of daring, like flying down the steepest mountain on a sled, or hanging out in the square to see who could impress the most girls. That's why I started talking to your mother," he conceded. "I was trying to impress my so-called friends, trying to prove myself as one of them. They dared me to go over and talk to her. Laughed at me and said I wouldn't have the guts, that I was too scared, too weak. So I did it."

His face went blank for a moment, and his forehead creased, as though trying to remember something important, something he couldn't quite grasp. Then he startled, like waking from a dream, and gazed at Astrid.

"Sorry for rambling."

Shaking her head, she mumbled that it was fine, but her mind was spinning. What had her mother been doing in that faraway village? Why had she really brought Finn here? And what had she told him – or done to him – to make him leave with her?

"So why did *you* stop painting?" Finn asked, dragging her back to the present again. Back to him.

Pain crossed her face, and she squeezed her eyes shut, trying to hide it. "I don't know," she whispered.

"Come on, what's good for the goose is good for the gander, right? Or something like that. I told you my embarrassing secret…" Finally catching sight of her face, he trailed off, then put down his brush and bridged the gap between them. "Hey, what's wrong? I'm sorry. Please don't worry, you don't have to tell me anything." He looked panicked as he reached out and squeezed her shoulder, and her heart ached for him.

Forcing a smile, she willed her tears not to fall. "I'd tell you if I could, but I really don't know. It wasn't until I showed you the art room, and saw the paintings, that I realised I'd once been artistic. That at some point I'd loved standing in front of a blank canvas, with all that amazing possibility right there before me, ready for me to create, and transform. To give physical expression to the pain and joy, and worry and fear, that I was feeling. To the confusion and self-doubt, and the love and loss."

Warmth flowed into her from where Finn's hand rested on her shoulder. And strength. Was it enough strength to face her own darkness though? Could she summon the courage to tell him what she'd done to Emilja? That it was her own fault the villagers hated her? Part of her wanted to confess, but she knew the look of horror and disgust on Finn's face if she revealed it would be too much for her to bear. Better that he like her, despite her lies and deflections, than to stomp off back home when he discovered the real her and rejected her completely.

"I love that we both love painting," Finn said, voice low and soothing. "I feel so much closer to you because we share this bond. And it means so much to me that you see the world as it could be, like I do, you see the potential. You understand me in a way that others can't."

His words thrilled her, and for a moment Astrid dared to consider a future with him in it. Then a knock at the door jolted her out of her reverie, and she cursed under her breath before grudgingly opening it. Kristina bustled in with a tray laden with thick beef stew and warm fresh bread, and she smiled gratefully as her maid set it down on the work bench then left them to it.

The spell had been broken though, and as they shared the simple, comforting meal, she and Finn spoke of less serious things. Time slowed as they returned to their canvases, sometimes in contemplative silence, at others full of laughter and good-natured teasing.

Finally, as the velvety night pressed in on them and they had to light more candles to illuminate the shadowy room, they declared their paintings finished. Finn darted over to see what she'd created – and gasped as he took it in.

"What's wrong?" Astrid asked, a quaver in her voice. When he didn't say anything, just continued to stare, she nervously made her way over to his easel, and gasped in turn. They'd both painted the same scene, just from different perspectives, of the two of them walking along the beach together, waves swirling around their ankles, and the sun setting in a blaze of golden light that had turned the twilight skies all shades of enchanted pink, orange, lilac and deepest mauve.

"I don't understand," she stammered, mind whirring. "How did you know?"

Their eyes locked, and Finn's eyes were wide with confusion. "How did *you* know?"

"Have you been to this beach?" she asked.

Finn shook his head, then blushed beet red. "I've been dreaming this scene every night since I arrived," he confessed shakily. "It's always a different time of day, but it's always the two of us on that stretch of sand. You?"

"Same," she admitted. "It's a dream I've been having since before you arrived. If I looked confused when we first met, that's why. I didn't think I believed in fate, or destiny, but surely this means something?"

Chapter 16

A rough hand on her shoulder dragged Astrid from a wonderful dream. She and Finn were on the ocean shore together, hand in hand in the sunshine, smiles wide, mood relaxed and carefree. Just like in her beach painting from the other day, which he'd deemed the winner of their contest. Sleepily she wondered what her prize would be.

She tried to slip back under into her dreamscape, but the hand would not stop shaking her. Cold and grumpy, she opened her eyes, and glared at Kristina. "Why did you bring me back here?" she muttered, pulling the quilts more tightly around herself in the grey, gloomy chill.

"I'm sorry, but I thought I should tell you. Finn woke up screaming this morning, and I just saw him on his way downstairs to see your mother. He looked really angry." The maid's voice shook. "I'm sorry if I should have let you sleep."

Rubbing at her eyes and trying to wake up, and make sense of the words, Astrid shook her head. "No, you did the right thing. Thank you for telling me. I'll go down and join them."

"Yes, my lady. I'll get your clothes for you while you wash your face."

Fear spurred Astrid on. Within minutes she was running down the stairs, long woollen skirt streaming out behind her. She tripped on the final step, and only just managed to catch herself on the banister before she fell.

She was so clumsy. Heat burned her cheeks, and she pulled herself stiffly upright. Her mother's cruel voice echoed in her head, all the insults she'd drummed into her over the past few years.

"A princess must be graceful." Said with a sneer, because clearly her daughter was not.

"A princess must be elegant." Snapped with a look of disappointment on her face that never failed to break Astrid's heart.

"A prince must be strong."

What?

The voice from her nightmares snaked out under the door ahead of her, and Astrid froze in horror. What was her mother doing?

Please don't let her be speaking to Finn.

As if compelled, she crept silently towards the door, bent her head to the keyhole and peered into the room.

Finn was sitting at the high table in a red velvet chair, his back to the door, his front facing the immaculately dressed monarch. How had her mother known to be up and ready so early this morning? It was still dark outside.

The Queen's mouth twisted impatiently, and venom dripped from her lips. "And a prince must be grateful."

Finn's head jerked up, meeting the cold, glittering eyes. "I am grateful, Your Majesty," he whispered, repressing a shudder. "I love being here, and I love your daughter."

Astrid gasped. *He loved her?*

"Then why do you resist me?"

He reached for something in front of him, and Astrid smiled, wishing she could see his face, his smile. Warmth filled her heart and radiated outwards, a shield against the bone-deep chill of the draughty stone hallway, the draughty stone palace, and her usually draughty stone heart. What she felt for Finn was completely new. It had terrified her at first, the sudden heat, and she'd worried that she was going to melt away to nothing. But she'd never felt better, or stronger. Never felt more alive. She was changing every day.

Was this love?

"Why?"

Her mother's harsh voice snapped Astrid back to the present, and she looked past Finn into her cruel eyes. What did she mean, resist her? What had she done?

"I don't mean to be ungrateful, Your Majesty," Finn began, voice trembling. "It's just that, well, I've been having these dreams that feel so real. I keep dreaming of a woman, old and kind, tucking me into bed. Of the deep love I feel for her, and her for me."

He paused, and tears thickened his words. "My... grandmother... perhaps?"

From the other side of the thick oak door, Astrid could hear his sadness and his longing. She couldn't imagine anyone feeling such love, but she knew it was real, because her own chest was aching and desolate in echo of his. A memory pricked at her. He'd mentioned his grandmother when he first arrived here. How long she'd cared for him, and how much he loved her. How had he forgotten her?

"And my best and dearest friend, Greta."

As he said the name, a vision slammed into Astrid and left her gasping for breath. A pretty girl with long golden hair, a constellation of freckles sprinkled across her nose, and kind green eyes. Eyes just like Finn's. She was standing in a summer garden in a flowing pink dress, flowers woven into her hair and reaching over her head. Jasmine vines curled from branches, reaching for her. Roses bloomed in every colour imaginable, cherry trees bent their boughs towards her, a bluebird perched on her shoulder – and Finn stood beside her, holding her hand, and gazing at her with an expression that brought tears to Astrid's eyes.

This was the girl she'd captured the shadow of in her portrait of Finn in front of his cottage. The next-door-neighbour who had given him the roses and, it seemed, her heart. How had she not realised this shadow would grow, and poison her? Poison her relationship with Finn? What was her mother doing to him? To her?

Had it ever been real between them?

Mocking laughter rang through the room and seeped out into the corridor where Astrid was still hunched, unable to look away from her keyhole view, even as her heart began to freeze, and to harden, back to how it had been before this sweet stranger had turned up at the castle and changed her whole world.

"Oh Finn, not those dreams again. They're just a silly fantasy, from one of those books you've been reading. Drink up, it will help."

Astrid watched in dawning horror as her mother nudged a glass of glistening dark purple liquid closer to him. Obediently Finn lifted it and drank its contents. Then he nodded. "You're right, of course I love your daughter. I don't need anyone else."

A self-satisfied smirk crossed the Queen's face. "Yes, you will make a wonderful co-regent and ruler when the time comes."

Through the blur of her eyes misting with tears, Astrid caught her mother's triumphant gaze, and crumpled to the floor, defeated. The last remaining warmth left her limbs, and she slid down onto the cold stone floor, hunched over and motionless.

Had that been a potion? Was this beautiful boy's affection for her solely because he was enspelled? It was one thing for her mother to somehow make him forget his past, but to actively shape his will and force him to like her was a step too far. She'd believed that he liked her, the vulnerable her, the artist her, the soul so like his own it felt like destiny. Was that all a lie?

Rolling her eyes, she laughed, a harsh sound. Of course that was the only way he could love her. Why would a normal human ever care about her, unless ordered to? The villagers hated her, and it seemed Finn would too, unless he was ensorcelled.

Hot tears dripped down her cheeks, and she burned with self-hatred. Those boys at the ball had been right. No one could ever love the daughter of the Snow Queen. She'd tried so hard to be good, to be better, to help those around her, but it was no use. She was destined to be just like her mother. Destined to *become* her mother. Bitter. Alone. Trapped in an endless winter for eternity.

The thought chilled her to the bone, and she crept back to her chamber, threw herself on the bed and cried.

The tightening in her chest intensified, and she felt her heart harden further, shrinking back to its stone-cold form, the way it had been before Finn's smile had pierced it with a warmth like sunshine and made her believe she could be loved. Now, it shattered into a million pieces, and she let the pain and darkness pull her under.

Weak light was streaming in the window when she woke up, hungry, thirsty, and hollowed out inside. Was it the same cruel morning, or had she passed out and slept for a whole day and night? The flashes of nightmares pummelling her brain pointed to the latter, but she couldn't bring herself to care. She just hoped her mother had already left the castle, because she never wanted to see her again. Never wanted to see anyone. She would stay in her room forever, until she wasted away to nothing. What was the point of living if she was fated to such a lonely, awful life?

And what *was* her mother doing when she was away from their icy home? Saving people's lives, or destroying them? She'd wanted to think she was helping, rebalancing the earth when the temperature climbed too high, when volcanoes exploded, when bushfires raged. But what if she was doing the opposite? Half-remembered accusations she'd heard whispered amongst the servants came back to her – avalanches, floods, strandings on mountains – and she wondered resentfully if they were right.

Pulling the quilt over her head, she vowed not to care. She couldn't save herself from her mother, so what hope did she have for protecting the whole world?

A tentative knock on her door shattered the silence, but she ignored it. And continued to ignore it as it became louder and more frantic.

"Go away Kristina!" she finally shouted.

It took her a while to understand the muffled voice, but when she did, a flutter of hope almost made her rise from the bed, before she sank back in despair. What could he want with her?

"Astrid, it's me, Finn. Can I come in?"

"No!" she screeched. "Go away!" She sounded like a harpy, vicious and hostile, which suited her mood perfectly.

"Are you sick?" he called back, worry in his voice. "What's wrong? Why didn't you come down yesterday?"

He almost sounded as though he cared about her. But no, it was just the potion talking. Finn was enspelled. Ordered to be her friend, to pretend he was interested in her. *Pretend he loved her.*

Her heart broke all over again.

"I'm fine. Just leave me alone," she snapped. There was silence for a while, and she tried to swallow back the disappointment that he'd given up on her so easily.

A hand on her shoulder made her jump, and she pulled the covers from her head in shock. Finn was peering down at her, green eyes sparkling with a light that still took her breath away. She was used to the cold, chilling blue eyes of her mother, echoed in her own face, and the depth of life and sunshine in this boy's gaze still moved her.

"Are you sick?" he repeated, concern clear in his voice. "What can I do?"

She wanted to reach out a hand to his rosy cheek, to wrap his warm arms around her and sink down against his strong chest. As though he'd heard her, he gently rubbed her cold shoulders, sending shivers of heat, and something else that she couldn't identify, through her whole body.

"Are you okay? Suddenly you don't look as pale as you did a moment ago."

A blush fanned across her cheeks, and against her will she smiled shakily back. "I'll be all right."

"Good. You were going to take me ice-skating, remember? You said as soon as the sun was out. Well, it's out! The minute your mother left this morning the clouds parted. Like magic!"

His mention of her mother brought the images of the conversation she'd witnessed between them slamming back into her, and she shuddered. There was no way she could be around Finn now she knew he only liked her because of a spell.

"Go away," she muttered bitterly. "I need to sleep, and you should be researching. That's why you're here, isn't it?"

He looked hurt, but swallowed it down and smiled an uncertain smile. "Come on, you promised you'd show me your favourite mountain run, and the frozen lake, and the mound where the foxes burrow. And I can't wait to see your snow-clad forest up close. Pretty please!"

His enthusiasm was catching, breaking down every excuse she had, and she wondered if it would be so terrible to spend one more day in Finn's company, pretending he liked her. Against her better judgement she managed a weak smile. "Fine. I'll meet you downstairs in half an hour."

As Finn eagerly left to get a thicker coat, all the warmth in the room went with him, and Astrid shivered. The face in her mirror smiled slyly at her, lips turned up in mockery, but she poked out her tongue at it and covered it with a long blue scarf, then headed to her bathing chamber to get ready. Once dressed, she grabbed her coat and ran downstairs. She knew it would tear out her heart when Finn left her to return to Greta, but there was no reason she couldn't enjoy his sunshine while it lasted.

Chapter 17

Climbing one last peak, their breath came fast and ragged, frosting in the icy mountain air like tiny snow angels puffed into existence just to float gently skyward. Astrid's chest was tight and hot with exertion and her heart thudded almost painfully, but she was exhilarated. Finn had kept pace with her the whole way up the mountain, and now that they'd finally reached the shore of the frozen lake, his cheeks were as red as hers, and his smile just as wide.

It was bracingly cold, but the sky was blue and the sun was shining weakly, and it felt so wonderful to be moving her body, breathing in the fresh, pine-scented air, and standing here with her friend, alone together, far from the shadow of the dark, dank castle and the foreboding presence of her mother.

She shook off the memory of the Queen's cold eyes and the purple potion she'd forced on their guest. Perhaps *that* had been the dream, and now she was here in the mountains, wide awake and all alone with Finn.

Finn who had begged her to come up here.

Finn who was staring at her with those kind, gentle eyes and a beaming smile. Had he brought the sunshine to her snowbound world, with his sweet innocence and optimistic personality? Was he the one who would thaw her frozen heart and bring warmth to her life?

And even if her mother had influenced his feelings for her in the beginning, couldn't she make him like her for who she was? Not because he was forced to, but because they were so perfectly matched, with so much in common. Because they got on so well, and seemed to bring out the best in each other. To see the depths they were capable of suffering, and encourage the highs too. He made her want to be the best version of herself, and surely that version of her was worth caring about on its own merits, no spellcraft or trickery necessary.

Her eyes drank him in as he moved ahead of her to the weathered grey bench. "My lady," he said with a bow, wiping the snow off the seat and placing his jacket down with a flourish.

Giggling, Astrid thanked him and sat down, and he settled next to her, a little closer than strictly necessary. Had he meant to? She peeked up at him under her lashes, searching for clues. Her body yearned to lean into his, but she felt shy around him now. Uncertain. As she bent down to lace up her skates, she froze every emotion she was feeling in her mind, a snapshot to pull out and re-examine later. She wanted to remember the carefree warmth of this moment forever, no matter what happened when they returned to the confines of the castle.

Beside her, Finn got to his feet on surprisingly steady legs, spun in a tight circle, then held out a hand to her.

"May I have this dance?"

Her jaw dropped. "I thought you said you'd never skated before." She couldn't mask her disappointment, but she tried not to sound too bitter.

"Well, I've never skated on a frozen lake on a mountain that pierces the heavens, but I may have tried it once or twice in the very provincial and only temporary ice rink in my village," he sheepishly admitted.

As she rose on legs stiff with reluctance, her heart sank. She'd been looking forward to teaching him how to skate, to having an excuse to hold his hand as he made his nervous way around the edges of the lake, and being the wise mentor as she guided his first steps. And, if she was brutally honest, she'd also wanted to show off her own skill and grace, and see the admiration in his eyes.

She wanted to dazzle this accomplished boy, but what if he was better than her on the ice? She couldn't remember the last time she'd come up here. How on earth could she impress him when he excelled even at this?

"Hey, I still want those lessons you promised," Finn said, lifting her chin with his gloved hand and staring into her eyes. "There's so much you can teach me, so just look at it as an advanced lesson, without all the boring keeping-me-on-my-feet bits."

His voice was flirtatious and his eyes were gleaming with mischief. She felt herself sinking into the emerald depths of his gaze, wanting to drown in the swirling ocean of his soul. The harsh cry of a bird overhead brought her back to the present, and she realised she was leaning into him, close enough to kiss.

Mortified, she jerked backwards, stumbling in her haste to put distance between them. Why couldn't she control herself? It was as though a magnet drew her to him, an irresistible pull she wasn't strong enough to break.

Frowning, she took another step away. Oh god. Her mother hadn't enspelled her too, had she? But she'd liked Finn from the moment she'd met him – and even before then, if her dreams meant anything. Spell or no spell, she loved who he was – his kindness, his personality, his passion for life and art and joy. She didn't need magic to make her care about this guy.

As though reading her mind, Finn clasped her hand and winked at her. "It's so cold up here. Come on, we need to warm up."

And in a flash they were on the ice, fingers entwined as they slowly got their balance and adjusted to the thin air so high up, and the momentum of their passage across the frozen surface. Finn took her in his arms in an echo of the waltz they'd danced at the last ball, and she smiled tremulously then closed her eyes, losing herself in his soothing embrace and in the sensation of his hand on the small of her back, and refusing to think of anything other than this single perfect moment in time.

It was so peaceful, she wanted to stay here forever, time stopping so they could be together always, cut off from the rest of the world, from who they had been before, and all the expectations and pressures of the future.

Sensing her shifting mood, Finn let his hand slip from her waist and linked their fingers again, then suddenly took off, picking up speed as they hugged the edges of the lake shore. Laughter trailed out behind them, and Astrid's heart flared again with hope when she saw the delight in his eyes.

"This is awesome!" he shouted.

Grinning back, she slowed them down with a slight pressure on his palm, then trailed a hand towards the ice, one leg out behind her, the picture of grace and elegance.

"You're so the princess right now," Finn called out, a smile in his voice. Then he copied her move, tugging briefly on her hand as he stumbled, but quickly rebalancing himself. Eyes sparkling, he whooped with joy. "See, you're a great teacher!"

She glowed at his words. "And you're a great student."

After a few more times around the lake, dipping and weaving, Astrid started to relax and enjoy herself. Thoughts of her mother, the village teenagers, and even her worries about Finn and what he thought of her, they all left her, and she basked in the gentle warmth of the pale sunshine, the sweet sound of Finn's laughter, and the sensation of his hand in hers. It was a balm for her frozen soul.

She didn't even notice that he'd picked up speed again – she was so happy to be in his company that she wasn't paying attention to anything else. Then her stomach tilted as he spun her towards him again.

Oh no! They were going too fast for this.

"Look out!" she shouted, but it was too late. As soon as their bodies made contact they were falling, and she scrunched her eyes closed and waited for the slam of her head against the unforgiving surface of the ice.

Yet it never came. Cautiously she opened her eyes. Finn had twisted himself beneath her and cushioned her fall, taking the brunt of the impact himself, and his face was deathly pale and still.

"No, no, no!" she called desperately, dragging herself up and onto her knees, and slicing into her thumb with the blade of one of her skates as she tried to steady herself.

Ignoring the trickle of blood, she stared down at her friend. "Finn, wake up! Are you okay? Please, you have to tell me, does anything hurt?"

Anxiously her hand brushed his pallid cheek, and she leaned over him, muttering to herself as she searched for a flicker of consciousness. He was lying motionless on the ice, unnaturally still, and her heart pounded with fear. What if he was seriously injured, so far from the castle, so far from help? She couldn't carry him back herself. Cursing under her breath, her mind spun in panic. She hadn't packed anything remotely useful, not even a blanket or a band-aid, and she doubted they'd survive if they were stuck in this frozen wasteland overnight.

What if he didn't regain consciousness?

She hadn't even told anyone where they were going. What kind of a ruler would she be if she wasn't even responsible enough for that? If she couldn't even keep her friend alive?

"Please Finn," she whispered. "Please don't be hurt. I promise I'll be more sensible, more caring. Emilja is right, I'm so selfish, and I don't deserve to..." Her words trailed off as a sob escaped her, and suddenly she was crying. Tears of worry and fear and guilt, all the pent-up pain and sorrow pouring down her face and splashing onto Finn's cheek.

He opened one eye and grinned impishly up at her. "I'll be fine, eventually. But I bumped my head really hard. Can you kiss it better?"

Relief stopped her tears, but she stared at him in shock. Did he mean that about the kiss, or was he mocking her? Or speaking gibberish because he was concussed, or another layer of the spell had been activated?

Oh, why had she brought him up here?

"Hey, I'm not that repulsive am I?" he asked, wounded. All signs of mirth slipped from his face.

"Oh, sorry, um..."

Reaching for her hand, he smiled sadly. "It's okay Astrid, you don't have to kiss me. I know I'm just a commoner to you."

"No, that's not –"

"And there's no need to worry," he added quickly. "I don't have any broken bones, just a bit of a dent in my pride, and perhaps a lump on my head. But it looks like I need that skating lesson after all. Come on, what do I need to know first?"

She tried to smile, but fresh tears stung her eyes. Of course she wanted to kiss him! How could he not know that? She'd been following after him since the day he arrived, all puppy dog eyes and admiration. Or was it desperation? The only reason she had hesitated was that she didn't know if he was just teasing her, or being nice because he was under her mother's spell, or if he was actually growing to care about her, to see the real her, beneath it all. Why were guys so infuriating? And why had her tutors never taught her about emotions and feelings, or how to read people? Surely that was just as important as maths, politics and geography.

Before she could get her whirling thoughts under control, Finn had managed to haul himself upright, and was helping her to her feet. Then he noticed her bleeding thumb, and his face flushed. "Did I cause that?" he asked, a crease of regret between his brows.

Astrid shook her head. "It was all me," she confessed. "I told you I was clumsy. And it's fine, don't worry."

Shaking his head, Finn lifted his jumper and tore a strip from the bottom of the shirt underneath, tenderly wrapped it around her wound, then pressed a kiss to her palm.

"Okay, I'm all yours," he said sheepishly, and turned himself over to her for the lesson.

At least she was familiar with ice-skating, which was far less shaky ground than the emotional wisdom she so clearly lacked. She showed Finn all the tricks and skills she'd taught herself over the years, masking her confusion and regret with practicality and constant movement. Slowly her embarrassment wore off, and she managed to stuff down the rest of her feelings. For today, she would enjoy his company, and refuse to look beyond these golden hours. She'd file these precious moments away to remember when he left her.

But oh, she desperately wished she'd kissed him when he'd asked her to.

The golden sun sank lower in the west, and the sky was emblazoned with streaks of pink, lavender and gold. A few light flakes of snow began to fall. Astrid sighed. She didn't want the day to end. Out here in the brisk, pine-scented air, away from the stuffy confines of the castle and her mother's overbearing, all-encompassing presence, she felt free, renewed. As though she could be exactly who she longed to be – the kind, sweet, fun person Finn liked. The girl he wanted to kiss.

The girl she wanted to be.

Skidding to a halt back at the bench, they reluctantly removed their skates, then Finn slung them over one shoulder, and their backpack over the other. "What are you thinking about, beautiful?" he asked.

Cheeks flaming, Astrid shrugged, trying to appear casual, unaffected by his presence, but her eyes were drawn to his mouth. As soon as she realised, she gazed down at the ground in horror, but not fast enough to miss the quirk of his lips as they curved upwards in a smile.

Why hadn't she kissed him when she had the chance? Cursing her stupidity, she turned towards home, and they cautiously made their way down the steep, slippery slopes, reminiscing about the day.

"My muscles are going to be sore tomorrow," Finn said. "But it was worth it! Can we do it again soon?"

Nodding happily, Astrid gazed down at the castle, each step towards it more unwilling than the last. It had been a wonderful day, despite his fall – and her regrettable refusal to kiss him when she had the opportunity.

"So who's Emilja?" he asked, breaking the comfortable silence between them.

Astrid gulped. "Who?"

Taking her hand, he drew her to a halt, and smiled sadly down at her. "When I was lying on the ice, you said Emilja was right, that you were selfish, but that's just not true at all. Whoever she is, she's wrong."

Hope fluttered in her chest. Could that be true? But Emilja's words from the night of the ball came back to her, and she slumped her shoulders in defeat.

"She was my friend, from down in the village, but..." she trailed off. A pain stabbed at her heart, and she felt the loss of her all over again, remembered the cruelty of her words like a physical blow. "I hurt her," she whispered. "But not nearly as much as she hurt me."

An icy blast of wind raged around them, the temperature dropped sharply, and the sky suddenly darkened. Shivering,

Astrid used it as an excuse to change the subject and hurry them along, wondering as she did whether her roiling emotions had brought the storm, or it was just a coincidence. Either way, they both put their head down and increased their pace, fighting against the strength of the gusts and eager to be indoors by the fire.

As they got closer to the castle, Astrid looked up to check the looming clouds. Peering through the snowflakes beginning to swirl around them, she saw a lone figure standing at the gates, staring up at the turrets, and shivering in a long cotton dress.

"Oh no! She has no coat, or shoes. Quick Finn, we have to get her inside or she'll freeze to death!"

She started running down the last hill, but stumbled and fell over in the hard snow. *Always the clumsy one.* Finn gently pulled her up, kissed her forehead, then took her hand before she could respond. "Come on, I think it will be faster, and safer, for both of us if I can keep you upright," he said, trying to sound serious, but failing.

Giggling, Astrid stared up at him, wanting nothing more than to fall into his arms, but the thought of the girl trembling in the snow spurred her on. "Believe me, I'd rather stay out here with you, but let's get her inside and warm, then we can head to the library and drink hot chocolate together by the fire."

His eyes sparkled in the dying light of the gloaming, and he sighed theatrically at her words, but nodded. Hand in hand they struggled against the thick blanket of snow on the ground, Astrid becoming increasingly anxious the closer they got. The girl was trembling with cold, and her bare feet were almost blue. It looked as though she hadn't brushed her hair in days, and the deep shadows under her eyes were like deep purple bruises. Her heart went out to her – until the girl's eyes widened with horror when she saw Astrid and Finn's fingers intertwined.

Who on earth was she?

The stranger glared at Astrid, then flew at Finn and threw her arms around him, pushing Astrid away. "I've finally found you!" she cried, not seeming to notice that he'd stiffened the moment she touched him. "We've been so worried about you, and it's been such a difficult journey to get here, but oh my god, you're all right!" She was tripping over her words in her haste and panic, until she finally drew a breath, and drew slightly back, drinking Finn in as a pale light flickered in her eyes.

Astrid stared at her with trepidation. Was this –

"I'm Greta," the girl said, reluctantly releasing Finn and extending her hand to Astrid. She took it, surprised by how warm her palm was, given her shivering.

"I'm Astrid, and this –"

"I know, it's Finn. I can't tell you how relieved I am to know he's okay. Thank you for keeping him safe. I was terrified that he'd frozen to death in the snow."

Finn was still staring blankly at the girl, as though he'd never seen her before, but Astrid felt all the joy and warmth of their afternoon freeze to ice in her veins, then seep out into the snow. If this was Greta – his best friend and possibly the woman he loved – she had no chance with him. Her beautiful vision of a life with Finn beside her turned to black and white, then broke up and faded away, a ghost dispersing back to a lost dimension.

Her heart ached, and she grimaced at the physical pain there, until a sharp gust of wind blew around them, cold fingers snaking beneath Astrid's layers of clothes and making her shiver. And if she was freezing, this girl must be close to death. The mystery, and the sadness, would have to wait.

"Come inside Greta, you need to get warm," she said, voice brusque as the fortress walls around her heart rose up again and slammed back into place. "We'll figure this out as soon as you've thawed a little and have had a hot drink, and something to eat."

Astrid tried not to notice the hurt on the other girl's face, and tried not to think too far ahead. She would deal with the practical stuff first, then she could break apart into a million tiny pieces.

Chapter 18

Bursting through the castle entrance, Astrid issued instructions to Kristina and the castle steward, a whirl of activity and efficiency as she tried to hold her pain inside and stop the tears from falling. A hot bath for Greta. Dry clothes. A chamber prepared. Hot food and hotter fire.

But once everything was in motion and her unexpected guest was being cared for, depression shrouded her like mist. She wandered into the library and waited anxiously by the hearth, freezing with a bone-deep chill despite the flames. The flickering orange tongues looked like dragons come to burn her to ash, and the injustice of finally finding love then having it stolen away raged through her.

Fists still clenched and stomach knotted, Astrid shook her head when Cook tried to make her eat, too upset to swallow anything. Then the door crashed open, and they both jumped. Greta, fresh from her bath and swathed in several layers of soft wool, rushed to the cheerful blaze and held her hands out to it, but the moment she smelled the food, she turned and pounced, falling on the bowl of hearty stew ravenously, as though she hadn't eaten for days. Maybe she hadn't.

Kristina, who'd been looking after their guest and had accompanied her to the library, ladled out a second bowl and sliced more of the warm loaf of bread, then whispered to Astrid that the girl was in a very bad way.

"Can you send someone down to fetch the doctor?"

"Already done, my lady. And I've made up the eastern chamber for Miss Greta, with extra quilts, and lit the fire. She'll sleep well tonight."

Absently Astrid smiled her thanks, then turned back to their guest. "Are you feeling all right? Do you need anything else?"

"This is the best thing I've ever eaten," Greta said through a mouthful, then swallowed and turned bright red. "Please excuse my lack of manners, it's been a long time between meals. I've been on the road for…" She broke off, and confusion flitted across her face, before she blinked and continued. "For a long time. Trying to find Finn."

After she crammed the last mouthful of stew and the last bite of bread into her mouth, she glared accusingly at Astrid. "Why is he here?"

It was Astrid's turn to blush. "I'm not entirely sure," she admitted. "Mother said he came to use our library for a research project, but he's been painting too."

"He's been painting?" Greta gasped, as though this fact was stranger than him being abducted to live in a palace. When Astrid nodded, her face softened. "I'd like to see them. He hasn't painted in so long. He kept complaining that he wasn't inspired enough. That there wasn't enough beauty around him to paint." She tried to hide the hurt this had caused her, tried to portray hope

the room, and his face lit up. "Come in, sit with me," he called out. "I'm so glad to see you."

Trying not to look too smug, Astrid moved to his side, the weight of her nightmare lifting from her shoulders as he stood up and drew her into his arms. His lips touched her forehead, and warmth enveloped her. It wasn't the passionate kiss she'd imagined on the lake, but it was a kiss. Her skin tingled where his hands rested, and she felt like she was floating, dizzy with relief at his public displays of affection, and reassured their connection wasn't entirely in her head. The fact that it must be driving Greta to distraction to see them so close was just a delicious bonus.

Maybe the girl's appearance would turn out to be a blessing. After her fears that Greta would steal him away, could she actually turn out to be the thing that would push him towards her, a subtle reminder of why he'd left home in the first place?

A discreet cough made Astrid draw back, embarrassment turning her cheeks red. Her maid was placing a fresh pot of coffee on the table, along with a jug of cream and a towering stack of pancakes. "Good morning, my lady," she said demurely. "You're looking radiant today." Then she turned to their guest, and politely asked how she was.

"I'm feeling better than I was," Greta said softly, as she moved sadly to the other side of the table so Astrid could sit with Finn. "Thank you for asking Kristina, and for your kindness last night."

The maid bobbed a curtsey and left the room, and Astrid took her seat next to Finn and gazed across at Greta, a pang of guilt engulfing her. The poor girl had nearly frozen to death on her doorstep mere hours ago. "I'm glad you're on the mend too," she said, contrite. "What would you like to do today? Do you feel up to a walk outside, or would you rather relax in the library by the fire?"

"I should look around, since I've never seen –"

Before she could finish, the castle steward silently entered the room, with an apology to Astrid for interrupting, and a message for Finn that the seamstress needed him for a fitting. Looking relieved for the distraction, Finn quickly stood, bowed to Astrid and Greta, then headed out the door, leaving them both staring after him.

"Can you show me Finn's paintings?" Greta asked the moment he'd left the room. "I have so many of them at home, but it's been a year since he painted, and I can't wait to see how he's developed as an artist with all the new inspiration here."

Astrid smiled sweetly. She couldn't wait to see the girl's face when she realised who had inspired them. "Of course, we can go as soon as you've had something to eat – you need your strength." She poured maple syrup over her pancakes then offered the jug to Greta, hoping the girl would be strong enough to travel home soon. *Alone.*

Savouring every bite of her breakfast, she examined their guest, sizing her up now she was warm and rested, and less bedraggled and beaten down. She was pretty, in a wholesome way, and seemed to be sweet natured. The scent of jasmine drifted around her, and Astrid had a vision of her in a floaty pink dress, long wavy hair flowing down her back, and flowers threaded through her hair. A girl of summer, Astrid figured, most at home walking barefoot in a garden, sun-kissed and followed by bees. This wintry kingdom must be hard for her to cope with.

Suddenly she realised the girl was speaking, and she jolted back to awareness of the room she was sitting in, and the situation she faced. "Thank you, that would be wonderful. And then I really need to talk to Finn. I'm not sure what happened to him to make him forget me. Maybe he had an accident on the way here..." She trailed off, looking just as sad and forlorn as she had the night before, when she was stranded in the snow.

For a moment Astrid felt a twinge of pity for her, and a wave of remorse washed over her, threatening to drown her. But she tried to tamp the emotions down. She'd fed and clothed the girl, and offered her shelter and friendship, but surely the rules of hospitality didn't demand she give *everything* of herself. And Finn was happy here. He'd been miserable at home, he'd said so. He'd wanted to travel away from his village, see new things, meet new people, become more than he was, so he mustn't care about Greta as much as she hoped. He *wanted* to stay here.

Hardening her heart, Astrid ate a final bite then pushed back from the table. She wouldn't let anyone steal Finn away from her, and the sooner Greta was aware that he'd moved on, and liked someone else now, the better. "Come on, the art room is on the next floor."

By the time they reached the top of the stairs, Greta was out of breath, her cheeks flushed from exertion, and another short sharp stab of guilt pricked at Astrid's heart. In her eagerness to prove her closeness with Finn, she'd forgotten the girl was weakened from her journey.

"Would you like to rest first?" she asked, but her guest took a deep breath, smoothed down her borrowed skirt, and shook her head.

"Okay then."

Opening the door with a flourish, Astrid couldn't stop a small smile at the shock on Greta's face. "Oh! They're, um, amazing." The girl walked closer, inspecting each canvas in turn, and Astrid gazed at them with her, remembering the stories Finn had told her while she posed for each one.

"He loves stories, doesn't he," she offered. "He's told me so many while we've been in here, tales of girls in red cloaks entering the deep dark woods, princesses sleeping for a hundred years behind hedges of thorns, witches in cottages on chicken legs, and maidens journeying through frozen wastelands to rescue their true love."

Astrid paused, startled. That last one felt too close to home. Greta had travelled across ice and snow to rescue Finn. There was a certain romance to that, and a level of sacrifice that was hard to comprehend. How much further would the girl go to prove her love? More frighteningly, how far would Astrid go to defeat Greta and win her beloved?

When she finally glanced back at her guest, Greta was nodding sadly. "Those are the stories his grandmother told us, while we were growing up. Stories show us who we are, and who we want to be. I'm glad he still remembers *them* at least..." Her voice trembled, but she continued pacing slowly around the room, looking at all the artworks – until she halted in front of the two paintings of Astrid and Finn walking along the beach hand in hand. "What –"

Astrid's cheeks flamed, and she felt less gleeful than she'd expected as she described how Finn had challenged her to an art competition, and they'd unknowingly painted the same scene. "We couldn't explain it, other than that it felt like fate. I'd been dreaming about us on that beach together before Finn even got here, and apparently he'd been having the same dream." The serendipity of that moment still awed her. "It all seems destined, don't you think?"

Greta shrugged. "I wouldn't know about that."

At the wall with the larger portraits, it was Astrid who gasped. There was a canvas she hadn't seen before, of her and Finn on the frozen lake yesterday – but in the painting his arms were around her, holding her close, her head was tipped back, and his lips were firmly on hers. So gentle. So sweet. And yet so full of desire and yearning too.

Her stomach tightened, and a wave of heat shot through her. It was exactly what she'd wanted to happen but had been too afraid to allow. Regret pierced her soul, but she tingled with anticipation too. Yesterday she'd been scared Finn was mocking her when he asked her to kiss him, but the passion burning between them in this painting clearly revealed how wrong she'd been. And it explained his absence once they'd brought Greta in from the cold too – he must have stayed up all night to paint this.

She leaned closer, noticing his hand in her hair, the closeness of their bodies, the way her own arm was crushing him to her, like she never wanted to let go. Longing seared her heart, and joy and excitement wrapped around her like a cloak of sunshine and starlight, all dazzling warmth and soothing comfort. Heat ignited in her belly, and for the first time in her life she felt beautiful. Accepted. Wanted. She yearned to go and find Finn right now, to throw herself into the circle of his embrace and drown herself in his kisses. Tell him that of course she'd wanted to kiss him yesterday, and she did today too, and would certainly still want to tomorrow.

But it was Greta's piercing gaze she felt, and she blushed, hoping her naked longing wasn't written across her face, as transparent as the cold air that suddenly surrounded them.

"I didn't realise things had gone so far," the girl said coldly, her words ice to the blaze of desire burning within Astrid.

Numbly she shook her head. "They haven't. I mean…" What did she mean? She certainly wanted it to go further, and now it seemed that Finn did too.

Greta scowled at her. "He obviously cares about you, and you've inspired him to new heights in his art, but it can't be real," she said scornfully. "There's something wrong here, like he's under a spell."

"Are you calling me a witch?" Astrid demanded. "There's no such thing as magic or spells." Her voice dripped with disdain, but she was scared Greta was right. What if it was just her mother's potion that made Finn care about her, and not the growing friendship developing between them, and their similarities and shared loves?

Her palms grew warm, and her hands pricked with energy. A vision of the moment she'd directed that strange energy at Emilja drilled into her brain, and she looked down to see a spark of electricity zigzag from her index finger. Horrified, she realised how easy it would be to unleash her powers and stop this girl in her tracks. To have Finn all to herself. It would harm Greta irrevocably, granted, yet she would win his heart.

Pulse racing, she plunged her hands into her pockets and turned away. For one wild moment she'd considered it, and shame drenched her until she shivered.

"Are you okay?" Greta asked, concern in her voice.

"Fine," Astrid rasped, heart still hammering, clenched fists trembling. "I just realised how cold it is, and you really should be resting. I'll take you back to your room, then I'd better get to the library. My tutor will be waiting for me."

And hopefully Finn would be too.

Chapter 19

Astrid made her way down to the library on unsteady legs, her mind whirling. Flashes of Emilja's face as she'd hurled her powers at her so long ago now mixed with visions of Greta with her hair standing on end and fear in her eyes. But she hadn't lashed out at her. She wouldn't.

Would she?

She paused at the library entrance, hand on the great oak door as she tried to compose herself. Inhaling deeply, she pushed all thoughts of Emilja and Greta away, and made her way to where her history tutor was waiting for her. She would be tested soon, and she needed to focus. Finn was nearby, continuing his research, and she smiled back when he waved at her, then studiously avoided him until her tutor finally left.

Night was falling outside, and when Kristina brought in their dinner she built up the fire to chase off the chill. Astrid and Finn sat together on a blanket in front of the flames, as they so often had, debating art techniques, sharing their hopes and dreams, and making each other laugh. Neither mentioned Greta, and Astrid was relieved that their guest had stayed in her room, and even happier that Finn hadn't asked after her.

But what would have happened if she'd unleashed her powers? It wasn't like she wanted to hurt the girl, she was just desperate for her to go away, right?

A tiny sliver of doubt tapped at her heart. "How would you describe me Finn?"

"What do you mean?"

Chewing her bottom lip nervously, she tried to keep the wobble from her voice. "Well, what sort of person am I?"

"You're lovely," he said, without a second of hesitation. "Sweet, polite, accomplished, welcoming. And you're a better ice-skater than me…"

"I'm serious," she grumbled.

Gently Finn took her hand and gazed at her. "I'm serious too," he insisted. "What is it Astrid? What's this about?"

"Am I a good person?"

"Of course! You're the kindest person I know. You care about people, whether it's a village in need, a girl lost in the snow, or me, not sure what I want to do or who I want to be. You motivated me to paint again, and helped me believe I could. You're talented yet humble, which is a wonderful combination, and you inspire me every day, making me want to be better, and do better, in the nicest possible way."

He smiled. "No one has ever believed in me like you do Astrid, or encouraged me to do what I want to do – or even asked me what that is! And no one has been as supportive as you are. You listen to me, and challenge me, and push me. You're the best person I've ever known."

Her vision blurred, and a single tear slid slowly down her cheek. "That can't be true."

"Cross my heart."

Wiping at her eyes, Astrid tried hard to smile. "Thank you. That's so sweet of you to say, even if it's a lie." She hiccupped, then when he started to protest, cut him off. "I'm not good enough, or strong enough, to one day rule this kingdom though."

Finn shook his head. "Nope, that's not true either. You'll be firm but fair. Compassionate as a strength, not a weakness. You see the good in people Astrid, like you did for me. They'll be lucky to have you as their queen. It's even a good thing that you're questioning yourself, because it means you won't be arrogant, or take it all for granted."

For a long time they both stared into the flames. Rather than reassuring her, Finn's words about her ruling made her shudder. She felt stupid, but somehow she hadn't properly grasped the reality of her birthright. Never actually believed she would one day succeed her mother. The woman of iron. The Snow Queen. Her heart pounded and her palms grew sweaty, body and soul rejecting the notion as panic and dread started swirling around her, trying to drag her down into the darkness.

"Do you think our lives are destined before we're even born, or can we change our fate?" she whispered desperately.

Finn turned to her, face softening as he drew her into his arms. "You're shivering. What's wrong Astrid?"

The care in his voice broke her, and she sobbed against his chest. As he gently stroked her hair, she realised she felt safe with him, able to be herself and speak her fears aloud. She'd never experienced that before. "I feel so trapped," she finally managed to choke out. "I can't rule a kingdom. Not by myself." Her voice cracked. "I feel so desperately alone."

"Hey, you're not alone. And while you will be a wonderful queen when the time comes, if that's what you want, you have to follow your heart. That's what you've been teaching me."

How could she not fall in love with someone who saw the best in her, a best she couldn't see herself? If only she could run away with him. Leave this castle, and her duty, far behind, and start a new life in the heart of some faraway city. They could find a little apartment in the artists quarter and paint all day, then spend their nights at exhibitions, or chatting in cafes with other creative souls, living their passion and their purpose, living their life. Not stuck here in some icy wasteland, with a mother who didn't even seem to like her. Like anyone.

"I wish I could," she said with a sigh. "But if nothing else, Mother has impressed the notion of duty on me. I'm afraid my destiny will trump my dreams every time."

"Is your mother really so bad?"

Astrid glared at him "You've met her. You've seen what she's like, how cold she is."

"Was she always like this?"

She opened her mouth, then paused. Closed it. Was she? "I don't know," she finally admitted. "It feels like she's never really been around, that I've been brought up by governesses and tutors, and by Cook and the castle steward. Mother always felt... remote."

"Do you think it was your father dying that did that? Is that what changed her?"

Her heart ached. She'd never known her dad, as he'd died before she was born, and she had no idea what her mother had been like before that. The Queen had always seemed so bereft of emotion and compassion, but she'd been young when her husband died. Had it been an arranged marriage, or were they desperately in love? For the first time, she wondered what it had been like to be suddenly widowed, suddenly a single mother, suddenly left alone to rule a kingdom. Had looking at her daughter made her ache with loneliness for her lost husband? Was that why she seemed to hate being around Astrid, hate spending time with her? Is that what drove her to travel so often?

Frowning, she tried to reach for a childhood memory, peering back through a swirling mist of shapes and moments, but there was nothing concrete. The paintings she'd seen in the portrait gallery didn't ring any bells either.

"A birthday?" Finn prompted. "Or a Christmas?"

She was standing at the foot of the stairs, wearing a bright red dress, her hair brushed until it shone and tied with green ribbons. Someone was holding her hand and leading her into one of the parlours, where a small, colourful feast was laid out, and a sweetly scented pine tree stood in a corner. Looking up, she realised it was the castle steward holding her hand and leading her to a pile of brightly wrapped gifts. Cook was sitting at the table with her son, smiling at her, and the housekeeper and her daughter Kristina were opposite, and waved at her too.

"Kristina was there," she whispered, but remained in the memory. "We were friends. And Cook was making sure we all had a happy day, even though she'd had no sleep, and had to organise this on top of all her usual duties. She baked my favourite cookies, and had managed to roast a small chicken and some vegies. But Mother wasn't there."

She paused, gazing around the room through her small self's tear-filled, disappointed eyes. Somehow she knew that Cook and the castle steward had found and wrapped those presents for her. She was about to return to Finn when a swirl of orange and nutmeg caught her attention, and she froze. The door swung open and the Queen strode in, wearing her travelling cloak.

"Festive blessings," she said sternly, then leaned down to kiss her young daughter's forehead. "I'm sorry I've been called away, but that's what duty means. You will be well cared for here." And she was gone. She hadn't even glanced at the people looking after her daughter.

Astrid's eyes snapped open. "She just worked all the time," she told Finn. "Even when I was tiny."

The memories came in a rush, crowding in on her, but they were all the same. No matter her age, she was surrounded by people who doted on her, but never her mother. When she did see her, the Queen was always alone.

"I don't remember her introducing me to a man, or ever being with one. How lonely she must have been." Tears stung her eyes, a strange mix of sympathy and quiet fury. "But I was here all that time. She didn't have to be alone."

It was too much. Her mother's callous disregard and Greta's accusations were daggers tearing her apart. She was going to shut down, overloaded and aching with a bone-deep fatalism that dragged on her body and soul.

Pleading exhaustion, she wished Finn a good night and stole up the stairs to her chamber. Now she sat huddled in the darkness, gazing out at the almost-full moon reflecting off the harsh white snow, her conscience pricking her. She loved Finn, and it seemed he cared for her too. But what if Greta was right and his feelings for her were only because of a spell. Could she survive knowing the truth?

Could she survive *not* knowing?

Chapter 20

A thin spear of pale light pierced through the gap in Astrid's curtains and forced her awake. She groaned, bleary eyed from too much angst and too little sleep.

Part of her wanted to burrow down under her quilt and hide in her chamber forever. Cosy and safe. Alone but unhurt. Everything felt too hard – winning Finn's heart, dealing with the unwelcome guest, making peace with her mother's emotional absence, and accepting that she would one day take her mother's place and rule this icy kingdom.

Another part of her was eager to seduce Finn into staying with her.

Dragging herself out of bed, she pulled on a lilac dress and slipped her favourite purple pendant over her head – then recoiled as she saw a flash of her mother pushing a glass of purple liquid towards Finn and forcing him to down it. Was it a spell, a curse or just a drink? And did he truly like her, the way she dreamed of, or was he just one more victim of the Snow Queen, bent to her will and stripped of his own?

The whole thing made no sense though. As she'd nudged the drink towards him, her mother had muttered something about Finn being a wonderful co-regent and ruler when the time came. What on earth did that mean? Co-regent how? What time? It didn't make sense.

Unless her mother was trying to set them up, but why would she do that? Did she think her daughter so incapable of ruling that she'd stolen a boy from his home to do it for her? Or was she actually trying to help her for once, to find someone to share the burden so her life was easier than her own had been? For some reason that possibility disturbed Astrid even more than her first idea.

Shaking off her thoughts and trying to bury her confusion, she headed downstairs to find Finn, and stopped in alarm at the dining room doorway. Greta was sitting alone at the long ornate table. The circles under her eyes were worse than Astrid's, and she was inexplicably struck with sympathy for the girl.

Reluctantly she took the chair opposite, and smiled as warmly as she could. "How are you feeling today? Did your rest yesterday help?"

"I think so," Greta said softly. "I'm still tired and weak, but it's amazing how much better I feel after eating such wonderful meals. Thank you for your hospitality, it's very kind of you."

Astrid shrugged, embarrassed. It wasn't like she'd welcomed the girl with open arms. And she should have. Wasn't that the first responsibility of the monarch and her family, to look after their people? "You're welcome to stay as long as you'd like, of course."

The girl smiled sheepishly, then took a deep breath, obviously trying to steel herself. "Look, I'm really sorry about the other day, when I was so rude to you," she said, words coming out fast, as though worried she'd lose her nerve. "Of course I don't think you're a witch, and I was completely out of line to suggest such a thing."

"It's okay," Astrid murmured, shifting uncomfortably as she recalled the power she'd wielded against Emilja, and come so close to unleashing at Greta. It seemed she *was* a witch, and her mother too. More Witch Queen than Snow Queen? Or some sad and twisted melding of the two?

"It's not okay. You welcomed me to your home, well, castle, and looked after me when I needed medical attention and could have died, and I was so ungrateful." Greta's voice trembled. "I suppose I was just hurt that you make Finn happy, and you inspired him to paint again, when I was supposed to be his muse but clearly couldn't do either."

She looked so devastated that Astrid just wanted to make her smile again. "It's fine, I promise. Now tell me about your journey here. And about your home. I've never left the kingdom." She paused. "Or this mountain."

"Never?" Greta asked, horrified. "Maybe I need to take *you* away from here so you can see the world."

A thrill went through Astrid at the very idea, even as she was rocked by fear. Could she leave the castle? Leave her home? Leave her mother?

Had she said that out loud?

Greta smiled. "Of course you can. Look at me. I'd never left our village before. It's a tiny hamlet, all the way across snowfields and mountains and a deep dark wood, at the other end of a mighty river surrounded by fields and flowers. I thought I'd never leave it either, that Finn and I would grow old together there, tending our garden, looking after our grandchildren, always dreaming of the big wide world, but never seeing it." She laughed. "Now I can barely remember the village, and can't imagine returning there, or settling down and getting married. The journey was terrifying, but it was incredible. And it changed me."

Astrid's mouth dropped open in shock. "Did you really travel down a river, and walk through a dark forest, and trek up and down mountains, and trudge miles across the snowy wastelands to get here?"

"Well, I had a bit of help along the way – a sled for a little while, and a princess's carriage, the cunning of a robber girl, a wise woman and a shaman, and for the last few days I was with a reindeer who let me ride on his back."

"Oh, it sounds just like a tale from a storybook!" Astrid exclaimed, eyes shining as her imagination ran wild.

Picking up her mug of coffee, Greta nodded wearily. "It felt like that at times, but it was a cursed quest, with one obstacle after another. There were many moments when I worried that I wouldn't survive, especially when I got closer to your castle and the going got really tough. People warned me that it's been winter here for two years."

"It has," Astrid admitted sadly. "Some strange never-ending winter we can't escape from."

Greta stared at her, entranced. "That sounds even more like a faery tale, all magic and romance!"

"It's not an adventure story like yours, and there's no romance to it, I promise. We really are cursed," Astrid said. But she didn't want to talk about that. Pouring more coffee into their mugs, she stirred in some cream and took a long sip of the thick brew. "Tell me about you and Finn."

"We've been best friends forever," Greta said, playing absently with her fork. "But a little while ago he started acting strangely. He withdrew from life, in a way. He didn't want to spend time with me any more, and he started answering back to his grandmother and being really rude, which is not like him, I swear."

"What happened?" Astrid asked. "Why did he change? He hasn't been like that here – he's so sweet and polite."

Pain crossed Greta's face, and Astrid cringed, suddenly, inexplicably, not wanting to hurt her. "Sorry."

Greta shrugged. "No one can work out what happened to him, or why. I know witches are only from faery tales, but it really did feel like he'd been magically transformed, changed completely from a sweet prince into a fearsome beast, and cursed to not be his true self again until someone made a sacrifice and turned him back."

Was that why Greta had set off on her journey, hoping it would be the sacrifice that returned her friend to her? Her heart must be breaking to realise it had all been for nothing. Finn still didn't remember her.

Picking listlessly at the fruit and nuts on her plate, Greta stared out the window into the blinding white snow and shivered, her face looking grey around the edges. The poor thing was no child of winter, and Astrid wasn't sure how safe it was for her to stay here. She needed sunshine and flowers, blue skies and warmth.

Surreptitiously wiping a tear from her eye, Greta continued. "Six weeks ago his grandmother came pounding on my door at first light, desperate to know where Finn was. He'd snuck out of bed during the night, and hadn't returned. We waited anxiously for two weeks, asking everyone in town, searching the countryside, and along the river. Most of the villagers thought he must have drowned, and told me to give up my quest and forget him, but I couldn't. Eventually one of his friends admitted that they'd all thought he was secretly dating an older woman, but hadn't wanted to say anything and get him into trouble. That's why it took them so long to come forward. After much begging, they finally revealed that they'd seen him climb into the luxurious carriage of a tall, black-haired woman swathed in white furs."

"My mother," Astrid whispered.

"What about me?" the Queen demanded imperiously, as she swept into the room in a swirl of robes, a flustered maid behind her. "And who on earth are *you*?"

The temperature in the room suddenly dropped, and ice formed on the windows. Greta's face turned white and she started shivering, from fear as well as cold. Astrid's gruff exterior cracked, and her heart went out to the girl.

"Hello Mother. You're home early."

Frowning, the Queen's attention shifted to her daughter. "I've returned for the winter solstice ball tomorrow night," she said icily. "I hope you have an appropriate new gown."

"Of course. I'd hate to disappoint you."

"Sarcasm doesn't become you," the Queen snapped. "Now tell me who she is."

Astrid smiled brightly, amused by her mother's discomfort. "This is Finn's best friend Greta. She's travelled through blizzards and across countries, all on her own, to find him and take him safely back home. Don't worry though, she'll look wonderful at the ball too."

The older woman shot daggers at their guest, and Astrid wondered what it was about the girl that was upsetting the Queen. Did she really want Finn to be with her daughter, or was the unexpected arrival of Greta disrupting her plans in some other way? Whatever it was, it had pushed Astrid firmly into Greta's corner.

Trying not to laugh, she stood up. "Come on, let's go and find you the perfect dress."

The two girls slipped out of the room while the Queen was still muttering under her breath, and headed up to Astrid's chamber. When she opened her wardrobe door, Greta sighed with pleasure and reached out a hand to stroke the soft velvet and tulle of the closest gown.

Astrid was relieved that she'd recently given most of her clothes away, worried that her companion would have thought her selfish and spoiled if she'd seen her former closet. But there were three new dresses, made for the recent balls, in addition to the three she'd kept, which probably still seemed excessive to Greta. She sighed. It was so strange seeing her life through someone else's eyes.

She had to think of herself though. Did she really want to help her rival look even more beautiful, more enchanting, more glamorous, and give her an advantage in the competition for Finn's attention?

Half an hour ago she'd wanted her gone, but when her mother had looked at Greta so disparagingly, Astrid had suddenly felt protective of her, eager to shield her from the Queen's wrath.

And now the conflict was eating her up. Who was she? Who did she want to be? Kind to the stranger girl, even if it meant losing Finn, or ruthless like her mother? What did she want – and what was she prepared to do to get it? How far would she go? Should she find Greta the prettiest dress, or the least flattering?

Before she could decide, Kristina bustled in, followed by the seamstress. "My lady, the Queen sent us, so we can alter one of your dresses to fit Miss Greta," Erika explained. "She said we'll need to take it in a little at the waist."

A wave of red-hot anger swept over Astrid, and she silently fumed. Her mother's humiliation of her wasn't complete? She had to insult her in front of the staff as well as her competition? Did she really hate her so much?

She felt a gentle touch on her arm, and turned to see Greta smiling ruefully at her. "These dresses would usually be too small for me, you're much more lithe than me, and far more graceful. But I walked for miles and miles a day on my journey here, and barely ate anything."

"Thanks," Astrid said stiffly.

Hunching down on her bed, hugging her knees to her chest, she watched as Greta tried on her dresses. The girl's face lit up with delight as she lifted the hems of silk and satin and spun around, the colour returning to her cheeks, and her shy giggle making Kristina smile.

Astrid glowered at them both. Part of her wanted to like Greta, to be her friend even. She was curious about her life, and her motivations. The bond she had with Finn, and the incredible journey she'd taken to get here. She'd walked for weeks through the snow to rescue him, the most incredible sacrifice, and act of love, that Astrid could imagine. And perhaps even more remarkable, and harder to fathom, she didn't seem to be bitter that Finn had forgotten her. Somehow she retained hope, and a kind heart.

But still the largest part of her wanted Greta to go back home to her village, and leave Finn for her. It was best for him anyway, as he wanted to be away from his village. He was happy here. And Astrid may feel the occasional pang of remorse, but she could bury that, she was sure, because she was determined to have him. Determined for him to be happy, and her as well.

Determined to win.

Spooning porridge listlessly into her mouth the next morning, Astrid ached with longing when Finn smiled at her. The way he looked at her, with such tenderness and respect, made her melt, and her resolve strengthened.

Surely it wasn't a bad thing to talk Greta into leaving, and Finn into staying? The girl *wanted* to go on another adventure, to head back out into the wide world and meet new people, while Finn was content to be here. If all Greta needed was to know that her friend was okay, then her mission had been successful. She'd found him, and seen with her own eyes that he was safe and happy in the castle, so she could be on her way now.

Feeling the other girl's eyes on her, Astrid faced her new friend, then a chill raced up her spine. Her mother must be behind her, standing in the doorway – she could feel her presence as a physical thing. And if she'd been in any doubt, Greta's terrified expression as she stared over Astrid's shoulder would have clued her in.

Sweeping in and taking her seat at the head of the table, the Queen offered a frosty greeting to her daughter and a warm smile to Finn, then turned to their guest. "So Greta, what brings you here?" she demanded.

The girl shrank in on herself, trying to appear smaller that she was. Trying to escape attention. Astrid recognised the movement, because she'd been doing it all her life.

"After Finn left home in such... mysterious... circumstances, I've been travelling everywhere, searching for him, trying to find him to see if he's safe and well."

"And is he, do you think?"

Finn peered intently at Greta, a frown of concentration creasing his forehead. His eyes were hazy, but a spark of recollection was beginning to shimmer across his face.

"I'm not sure," Greta said hesitantly, smiling at Finn with a sad, wistful expression.

"Well, he seems fine to me," the Queen snapped. "And have you seen his paintings? He's an incredible artist. So inspired. He told me he hadn't been painting for some time before he left home, and surely that's a crime for someone so talented. Obviously he would be better off here, where he's nurtured and valued fully. Where he has every opportunity to fulfil his potential."

Reluctantly Greta nodded, even though it hadn't been a question, then gazed down into her lap, defeated.

The Queen smiled haughtily. "Well, there's your answer. Now, coffee?"

Coffee. Was it an innocent drink that fought off the icy chill in the air and imparted energy and strength, or a wicked potion that stole people's memories? Could *it* be the thing that had made Finn forget his dearest friend, Greta overlook Astrid's malice, and her maid deny she'd ever stayed with her in her chamber and discussed time loops and eternal winters? Was it the reason Astrid had forgotten her friend Emilja, and the harm she'd done her?

Watching her mother pour the thick black brew into Finn and Greta's cups, a lead weight settled in her stomach. It was crunch time. Did she pretend ignorance of her mother's spell, take Finn's hand, claim his heart and command Greta to leave? Or should she do the right thing, tell them not to drink it, and curse herself to a life of loneliness and heartbreak?

Distraught, she pushed back her chair and fled.

Chapter 21

A knock on Astrid's door made her heart race. Was it her mother, come to berate her further? Greta, demanding to know what was going on? Or could it be Finn, ready to swear his love – or tell her he despised her and was abandoning her, as she'd always feared?

All day she'd been sitting in the window seat, shivering with cold, trembling with trepidation. Peering out at the pine trees as they danced in the gale force winds, casting eerie black shadows like bone auguries across the snow. Gazing mindlessly at the relentless, endless blizzard, desperate for someone to reveal her future.

But now the moment was here, she suddenly didn't want to know.

The knock grew louder, hammering into her skull in time with the beats of her aching heart. Then the handle turned, the door creaked open, and Kristina tentatively poked her head in. "May I come in, my lady?"

Scrubbing at her eyes, which stung with the heat and salt of her tears, Astrid nodded reluctantly.

Her maid entered the gloomy chamber, then motioned to someone still standing in the corridor. She looked nervous. "The ball starts in half an hour, and the Queen is demanding your presence." Her soft voice shook. "And, um, she said you would have some jewellery that your guest could wear?"

It was Greta hovering in the doorway, looking like she'd rather be anywhere else. Astrid knew the feeling well. "Mother believes we should both be there tonight?"

"It seems so," Kristina said, voice uncertain, and visibly uncomfortable as the go-between.

Bemused, Astrid beckoned Greta into the chamber and pointed her to her silver jewellery box, then allowed her maid to help her into her new ice-blue dress. Once poked and prodded and tightly laced up, she sat unblinking at the dressing table as Kristina powdered over her swollen eyes without comment, added colour to her pale cheeks, then arranged a wreath of flowers and berries that matched her dress atop her pale hair. She felt strangely disassociated, not fully in her body. As though she was watching from a great distance as her mind warred with her heart.

Finally she glanced up and saw Greta, the epitome of summer innocence in her floaty pink dress, with flowers woven through her untamed golden locks, her cheeks flushed rose-petal-pink with excitement, and her eyes now sparkling with anticipation.

Astrid's heart ached, her stomach clenched, and the bitter taste of envy was sour on her tongue. Once she would have wanted to be this girl's friend, but now she just wanted everything she had – hope, freedom, and Finn.

Jealousy pushed her to her feet, and she drew herself up to her full height and tried to gather the tattered wisps of her confidence around her. It didn't work. Her legs were heavy with dread, and the familiar weight of inadequacy dragged her towards the icy stone floor. She just wanted to hide. To fade away and be invisible again.

Instead she tried to channel her mother. Lifting her head in the same haughty way the Queen did, her back ramrod straight and her expression cold and remote, she squared her shoulders. She thought of all the conversations she'd had with Finn, all the things they'd shared, and all the compliments he'd paid her. Even if it *was* a spell that had brought him to her, was that so bad? She wasn't just a princess, she was also an artist, like him, and perhaps most importantly, the person who believed in him – the only one who did, if he'd spoken truth. Greta was just an old friend, a part of his childhood, someone he'd outgrown.

Wasn't she? Couldn't Astrid be his present, and his future? She could certainly make it worth Greta's while to bow out, if it came to that.

Feeling magnanimous, she thanked Kristina, then ushered Greta out of her chamber and down the wide stone staircase to the ballroom. She glanced at the girl and smiled. They were summer and winter in their pink and blue dresses. Flowers and berries. Sunshine and gloom. Finn's childhood best friend and his future love, she hoped.

Pushing the heavy oak door open, the two girls entered, and a hush fell over the room. The music stopped, and everyone turned to stare at them. Astrid inclined her head politely as women in scarlet red or emerald green gowns and men in richly coloured velvets paraded up to her to pay court, yet her eyes wandered restlessly, seeking Finn.

As the orchestra started back up, Greta was also gazing around the room, wide-eyed with wonder.

"Has it always been like this, people curtseying to you, seeking favour?" she asked, watching the castle steward as he supervised the formally dressed waiters carrying trays of sparkling drinks and tiny but exquisite appetisers. Popping a golden pastry into her mouth, she groaned with delight. "Have you always had so many servants?"

"No, of course not!" Astrid said quickly, defensively, her borrowed glamour sliding from her skin in her agitation. As her shoulders slumped, she saw herself through Greta's eyes – spoilt, privileged, undeserving – and didn't like it one bit. Not just because it wasn't how she saw herself, or how she wanted to be seen, but also because it wasn't true, and the injustice burned within her. "Most of the time it's just Cook, Kristina, the castle steward and the stable manager. Mother travels a lot, so I spend all my time with tutors. Or alone. That's why it's been so wonderful having Finn stay."

She paused. That wasn't the whole truth of why she loved Finn being here, but she wasn't going to confess the rest of it to this girl. Or to anyone.

There was sympathy in Greta's eyes as she took a sip from her glass and scrutinised Astrid. "That must be tough. I don't know what I'd do without Helga – that's Finn's grandmother. She basically raised us both, and I've never felt lonely for a moment. Never doubted my place in the world. Well, until Finn left us."

She swallowed another mouthful, and her eyes clouded over, confusion drawing her brows into a frown. Then her gaze cleared and she took in the room again. "Sorry, what was I saying?"

Heat flooded Astrid's cheeks. Was *every* drink enspelled? "Something about Finn's grandmother," she mumbled.

They were interrupted by a trumpet blast, and the Queen entered the ballroom to the sound of applause and the shifting of feet as people parted to allow her through. As her mother made her grand entrance, Astrid didn't watch her. Instead she studied the people around her. They were smiling at their monarch, but it was a little too reverential. Obsequious. And beneath the forced gaiety, there was fear on their faces. They trembled just a little as their ruler glanced at them.

Feeling eyes on her, Astrid turned to see her mother staring at her, expression cold, brittle, challenging. A shiver raced up her spine. This woman wasn't just the Snow Queen, she was the Ice Queen too.

Yet for just a moment Astrid saw a crack in the mask her mother wore. Saw the depth of her sadness. Her loneliness. She gasped. Her mother was lonely? She always acted as though she was so far above everyone else. So superior. But could her aloofness be a protective mechanism? Did she push people away before they could reject her?

Why *had* her mother never remarried? Never even dated? Had she made everyone forget what mattered most to them because she didn't want to remember her own loss?

Astrid's jaw dropped as she saw the vulnerability, and her heart ached. Was her mother just as lonely as she was?

But as soon as the thought flitted through Astrid's mind, the Queen's face transformed, and she was the cold, calculating ruler again. Had the whole vulnerable thing been a trick of the light, or a manipulation to win her over? She almost laughed. The Queen always got what she wanted, but at what cost? She was feared by her people, feared by her staff.

Feared by her daughter.

Did she want that for herself? To be intimidating and selfish like everyone expected her to be? She could stay silent and take advantage of Finn, pretend she didn't know there was a spell, but that would just prove she was the same as her mother. Just as heartless and harsh. It might be fitting, if she was to inherit a kingdom of ice, but she wanted a life of summer, not winter. Of sunshine, not storms. Of love and friendship, not cruelty and despair.

It would tear her apart, but she had to confess what her mother had done, and relinquish her claim on Finn's heart. Had to let him be with Greta.

"It's such a magical night," the pink-clad girl said, eyes alight with mischief. "You could almost believe a witch lived right here in this faery-tale castle."

Astrid nearly choked on her drink. "So you do know."

The orchestra started playing a lively waltz, and people shifted around them, the candlelight bathing them in a soft golden glow.

Greta tilted her head and smiled as she regarded the girl in blue, who shifted uncomfortably as her soul was laid bare. "I know how much Finn likes you."

"I wish," Astrid muttered. "It's you he should be with, but he doesn't even remember you, thanks to my monster of a mother and her wicked spells."

A laugh tinkled from Greta. "He remembers me just fine. We spent the day together today, and it filled my heart with joy to finally understand how happy he is. And I was able to share with him what I've been discovering about myself and what I want too."

Astrid grimaced, but made herself speak. "But you love him, and he loves you. I won't come between you – it's obvious you're supposed to be together."

"Says who? Certainly not Finn – we've been talking since you ran out at breakfast this morning, in a way we never have before. Yes, when I set out to search for him it was because I loved him and had always assumed we'd be together. And I admit I was wildly jealous when I saw you both holding hands that first day, and was desperate to win him back. But I learned a lot about myself on this journey, and realised that the only reason I thought I'd be with Finn forever was because other people expected it."

A nervous waiter approached the girls and offered his plate of mini puff pastry pies. Astrid shook her head, too apprehensive to swallow a thing, but Greta quickly ate one, sighed with pleasure and took another, then returned to her story. "Sorry, these are just too good! But back to me and Finn. Ever since we were kids, everyone in the village said we'd marry, like it was inevitable, and I never thought to wonder what *I* actually wanted. I only ever saw myself as a reflection of him. I was just half of Finn-and-Greta, never myself. No one saw me, or asked what I wanted."

She looked sad for a moment, then sipped her drink and grinned. "It's not Finn's fault that I thought it was preordained that we'd one day wed – he'd fallen into the trap too, under the crushing weight of other people's assumptions. Neither of us imagined anything else was possible, which seems so bizarre now."

"But what changed?" Astrid whispered, almost too scared to ask. Too scared this girl might change her mind if she was reminded about her childhood sweetheart, and the expectations of an entire village. She pictured Kristina's mother, tough and resourceful and pragmatic, determined to do what was best for her children, even if it meant she barely saw her oldest daughter. What would happen to

Finn's grandmother if he stayed here? "You just said you still thought that way when you got here."

Greta laughed, then drained her glass and allowed a hovering waiter to refill it. "Travelling on my own was the best thing I ever did, although I guess it took a bit longer to actually embrace everything I learned, and work out what it meant. Finn and I both desperately needed to expand our horizons. Learn who we were without the other."

Pain crossed her face. "In the deep dark woods I faced my shadow self, stared down my demons, was challenged on everything I've ever believed, and discovered so much about myself. I realised I don't want to settle down in a small village, I want to explore the world. Meet people, see things, experience other places and cultures."

"But if the spell has been broken, and Finn remembers now, it's because of you," Astrid forced herself to say. "You're the one who made the sacrifice, walking for weeks and weeks in the wilderness to rescue him, like the girl in the faery tale whose beloved had been stolen away and transformed into a bear, and had to trudge across snowfields and up mountains of glass to rescue him."

The scent of cinnamon and nutmeg from the candles swirled around the two girls, cutting them off from the rest of the guests. "No," Greta said. "It's you who made the sacrifice that brought Finn back to himself. Your decision this morning, just before you fled from the dining room, is what dispelled any lingering forgetting."

Astrid shook her head. She hadn't made a decision. She'd wanted to cry out, to warn them not to drink the coffee, had known it was the right thing to do, but she'd remained silent. She'd been selfish, and cowardly, and thought only of herself. "I didn't choose," she admitted, voice thick with remorse. "I knew what I *should* do, but I didn't do it. And I've hurt people. I almost hurt you." She cringed as she remembered the feeling in her palms as the power had gathered to strike out at Greta.

Crushed by the weight of regret, she turned to leave, to escape again and hide herself away. But Greta grabbed her hand, anchoring her where she was, in this room of rising heat and colour.

"No," the girl repeated. "I saw the moment your heart decided, even if it took your head a little while to catch up. Despite your feelings for Finn, you were selfless enough to give him up if that's what made him happiest, and that's a rare quality. But even before that, you gave him back his art, and inspired his creativity. You shared your dreams with him, and encouraged him to dig deep to discover his own. I know this is true because he told me! And I'm sorry that I was so selfish and quick to dismiss you when I arrived. I was jealous, not just about how much Finn cares about you, but of your life."

"There's no need to envy me this life," Astrid muttered.

Her new friend put an arm around her shoulder, and smiled gently. "I know that now, and I apologise, I had no idea. I just assumed you would be stuck-up and shallow, and that Finn could only have fallen for you because of a spell, or from coveting your life – or your library."

They both grinned this time. It *was* an amazing library.

Astrid was overwhelmed with sudden hope. Could it be true that Finn wanted to stay? Wanted to be with her? For a moment she allowed herself to wonder at the possibilities. At the kind of life they could have together. Then she inhaled sharply. Finn was standing in the entrance to the ballroom, looking for...

Was he looking for her, or for Greta? Her heart sank.

"But you love him," she said sadly. "You can't just stop loving someone." It seemed her mother never had.

"I do love Finn," Greta conceded, and Astrid gasped as the last speck of hope deserted her and her frozen heart shattered into a million tiny pieces.

Had this all been a trick, some kind of payback from Greta? But she quickly continued. "Only as a friend though! I met someone on my way here who I'd like to see again. I realised I just want as many adventures as possible, and what could be better than a winter solstice ball in an enchanted castle?" Greta beamed at her. "So I'll be leaving tomorrow, and I wish you and Finn nothing but joy, creativity and inspiration."

Astrid sighed. It couldn't be that easy. She ducked her head, hoping Finn hadn't spotted them. Maybe she could sneak out the side door and head back to her chamber, and lock herself inside until the two of them left.

"That's lovely, but it doesn't change the fact that Finn is in love with you, and that he only likes me because of a spell. I can't come between you, and..."

She held up a hand when Greta tried to protest. "And I won't be someone's second choice either. If nothing else, Finn has shown me that I deserve more than that."

Chapter 22

Greta's laughter rose above the sound of the orchestra, and several guests turned to gawk at the two girls before returning to their conversations. Her expression of joy also attracted Finn's attention, and he waved and started threading his way through the crowd towards them.

Astrid blanched, but Greta took her hands and stared into her eyes. "That coffee 'spell' of your mother's? It was just to help us survive the unnatural cold of this endless winter. You've been cooped up here for too long on your own, you're imagining things. I've spent the whole day talking to Finn, and it's not me he loves, it's you. You're the one who believed in him, and inspired him, and who makes him happier than I've ever seen him. And it was your kind heart that made him fall for you, not trickery or magic. Kindness can counteract any spell. So please, go dance with him!"

Before Astrid could make sense of the girl's words, Finn had reached them, and was offering her his hand again. A small part of her was still terrified that he was playing with her, mocking her in some way, but Greta nudged her towards him, and she decided it was time to be brave. Even if it was a joke, surely it was better to take that risk for the chance of a happily ever after, no matter how slim, than to live her whole life wondering "what if?".

Taking a deep breath, she forced her feet towards him. She was shaking – with nerves, and excitement, anticipation, and fear – but when he smiled at her, a question in his eyes, she reached out and took his proffered hand, and the look of relief on his face made her melt. Maybe he was just as scared as she was of being vulnerable, of exposing his true self, and of being rejected.

The music swelled, and Finn twirled her around then spun her back, right into his arms. Gazing up into his eyes, those kind eyes that had enraptured her the first day they met, she saw sunshine and laughter swirling in their depths. Saw possibility and potential, and fragments of a future that filled her heart with joy.

"I wasn't sure you were going to take my hand," he whispered, soft breath on her cheek.

Her voice shook. "I wasn't sure you were going to offer it."

Raising his other hand, he gently cupped her face. "How could you doubt that?"

She didn't want to say it, was terrified it would ruin everything, yet she had to know. Really know. "Um, because of Greta," she mumbled. "The one you've always loved?"

The intensity of his gaze increased, burning into her and illuminating the darkest parts of her soul. "Greta has been my best friend since we were babies, but that's all we are. Like sister and brother. It was you who saw something in me that no one else did. You who inspired me to paint again, and to connect with my heart and my true self."

He ran his thumb delicately over her cheek. "And everything you brought out in me, it's all for you. You make me want to be a better person Astrid, to be kinder and braver, and I can never repay you for that."

Vehemently she shook her head. "You've got it all wrong Finn. You don't owe me anything – it's me who is in your debt! You're not just my best friend, you're my only friend. You've helped me see a world outside of this castle, outside of this life, and most importantly you've seen *me*. You've encouraged me to find myself, and my freedom. The me you claim to care for so deeply only exists because of you. Before you came here, I was lonely and sad and resentful. And bitter and selfish and uncaring," she confessed, shame making her voice low.

"I don't believe you," he said simply. "You *do* care about people, and you need to trust that they care for you too."

His words were a balm for her sore and weary heart, and she smiled in gratitude. "You are so sweet."

Outside, lightning flashed, illuminating the ballroom with shimmering bolts of electricity, then thunder crashed overhead. Hail poured down on the roof and pounded against the tall windows, and people winced, muttering about relentless evil weather and endless rain and snow.

Astrid shivered, then raised her voice so she could be heard over the violence of the storm. "And you've put up with this never-ending winter, which is admirable."

"I'd put up with eternal night if it means I can be with you," Finn said softly, lips at her ear. Then he leaned in closer, voice crackling with raw emotion. "I love you Astrid."

And then his lips touched hers.

Time stopped. It was the lightest, sweetest kiss, full of sunshine and tenderness, innocence and desire, and a promise that she would never be lonely again. Astrid's pulse raced, and the dance of butterflies in her stomach intensified. She was floating, unmoored from her life, from her self, and yet she felt *more* anchored, and *more* safe, than ever before.

The music swelled in time with her pounding heart, then there was a sudden silence as she surrendered to the enchantment swirling between them. "I love you too," she murmured. She drew back and gazed up at him, drowning in the beauty of his gold-flecked eyes made a deeper green by desire, the warmth of his flushed cheeks, the smile that made her quiver with want, and the relief that she'd said those words back to him etched across his face.

Then his mouth claimed hers again, more demanding this time, and her knees weakened. Flooded with heat and wild abandon, she pressed her body harder against his, loving the way his fingers twined in her hair while his other arm crushed her against his solid chest, their closeness comforting and dizzying at the same time.

Their breathing synched, and Astrid's lips parted. Her arms tightened around him, suddenly possessive. She was intoxicated by the taste of him, the scent of him, and she marvelled at the heat between them.

They would be able to survive this eternal winter, with the warmth and passion their embrace generated.

The thought made her smile, and she pulled back slightly to peer up at him and convince herself that he was real.

Finally she noticed the dead silence in the room.

And the light. Staring around in shock, Astrid wondered if their kiss had transported them somewhere else, because the storm-darkened night had disappeared, and the first rays of a spring dawn were shining in through the floor-to-ceiling windows. Everyone was rushing over and touching the glass, rubbing their eyes in disbelief, wonderstruck by the vivid blue sky and the emerald-green grass being revealed as the snow melted away to nothing.

"You did it, Daughter," came a voice from the entrance, and every guest turned as one to see the Queen sweep into the room, smiling triumphantly. Next to her was Emilja, her long loose hair its original deep red colour, her face wreathed in a radiant smile.

Astrid's mouth gaped and she trembled with shock, but Finn had his hands on her shoulders, supporting her, caring for her, as he'd promised to do.

Her mother met her in the centre of the ballroom and smiled imperiously, then glanced at Finn with a knowing look. "Darling, the snow curse was triggered when you hurt Emilja – that's what plunged us into this two-year winter. Only you sacrificing yourself for someone else could break the cycle of eternal winter, and in giving up your claim on Finn's heart despite the depth of your feelings for him, you balanced the scales. And so spring has arrived at last. I'm so glad that you two have woven your hearts together after all."

Astrid's face grew hot with embarrassment, but the Queen was pointing towards the windows, and all the guests looked that way again, just in time to see the fiery golden ball of the sun rise above the horizon.

Cheers rang through the air, and people flooded outside to stand on the grass, laughing with joy, relief and exhilaration as the sun's rays warmed them.

"And I'm sorry Greta, but Astrid was right about the coffee spell," the Queen admitted once the room was deserted. "It wasn't to protect people from the cold, like I told you, it was to make everyone forget."

Surprise and anger flashed across Greta's face, and Astrid's heart clenched in pain. She'd had happiness in her grasp, real happiness, but her mother had just wrenched it away from her. She'd known it was too good to be true.

But the Queen had tears in her eyes, and they welled with remorse. She reached out to her daughter with desperate hands. "It wasn't malicious, I swear. I just wanted to take away all the pain and grief, stop the hurting. I was still so broken from the loss of my husband, and the thought of losing you too, to your pain over hurting Emilja, was more than I could bear." A tear slid down her cheek.

"So I made people forget, made *everyone* forget. You, your friends, the castle staff, the villagers, even Finn. But I didn't realise that in turning off the bad memories, I was erasing our most precious ones as well. Erasing *everything*. You forgot how much I loved you, how happy we'd been together, even the painting that had been so important to you. All because I was too scared to remember my life, and my love. Too scared to remember *me*."

The pain of all that had been lost was pulling Astrid undone. It was hard to believe the Queen was so sad and broken by the loss of her husband so long ago that she'd magicked an entire kingdom into forgetting – but if Astrid's pain at losing Finn now, after such a short time together, was any indication, she couldn't even begin to comprehend the depth of her mother's despair. Guilt bubbled up in her, that her own error of judgement had forced her mother to cast an even deeper, darker spell. What a burden she'd taken on, to save her daughter. What a power she had.

"Yet I started remembering," she whispered, thinking of the paintings she'd seen that showed the relationship they'd shared – a relationship that had been torn apart by magic.

"Yes," her mother admitted. "I think your recall began when we ran out of coffee for those two weeks, but your feelings for Finn worked against the magic too, cracking its power over you. It just took me a while to figure it out, because along with everything else, I'd also forgotten that I'd cast the spell." The Queen laughed mirthlessly.

"But why did you even bring Finn here?" Astrid asked.

For a moment her mother's eyes blazed with the fire of the northern lights, greens and mauves deepening her icy blue gaze as she turned to their guest, who was still standing behind Astrid, his arms around her.

"Because he'd forgotten himself too," she said softly. "Before he ever met me, he'd been cursed to forget how important his friend Greta was to him, and the love of his grandmother, even his connection to nature and the world."

Astrid turned to Greta, an eyebrow raised in question, and she nodded sadly. "It's true. Finn had always been so kind and considerate. He cared about me, and his grandmother, and looked after her – until all of a sudden he changed, ignoring us, and leaving her alone all the time. He used to love our garden too, and the magic and wonder of the world, but he rejected that as well – he pulled the plants out of their pots, told me I was a baby to care about them, yelled at his grandmother, and refused to do anything she asked. Sorry Finn," she said, clearly distressed to reveal this truth, but he just shrugged and smiled sadly at her.

"That still doesn't explain why you brought him here though," Astrid said to her mother, taking Finn's hands protectively, trying to let him know she was on his side.

"There was still a tiny spark within him that nothing could extinguish, and it was that dim light that called to me. At the time I didn't know why – I just wanted to bring you a friend, someone who would love you for who you are. You were so upset after your first ball, and it was killing me to see you so sad and lonely."

Emilja shuffled uncomfortably next to the Queen, and smiled tentatively when Astrid suddenly glanced at her, remembering she was there. "I'm sorry we were all so cruel to you that night," she said hesitantly. "And, um, at school. With Kye. I betrayed you."

Shaking her head emphatically, Astrid took the girl's hands and bravely met her eye. "It's me who needs to apologise. I really regret that I hurt you." She tried not to look at her vibrant red hair, which tumbled in loose curls around her shoulders and down her back, a beacon to remind her of that angry power she'd tapped in to on the school steps. "I hope that one day you'll be able to find it in your heart to forgive me."

Tears welled in Emilja's eyes as she threw her arms around Astrid. "Of course I forgive you, if you can forgive me?"

When Astrid nodded, the other girl grinned, said she'd return to see her the next morning, then ran outside, desperate to join her friends in the glorious sunshine.

The Queen smiled, the first genuine smile her daughter could recall, and a wave of relief swamped Astrid. Her legs shook, and her mind spun. She needed to sit down before she fell down, and embarrassed herself even further. As though he'd read her mind, Finn slipped his arm around her shoulder and pulled her into the warmth and security of his embrace. His eyes were shining like stars as he looked at her, filled with kindness and compassion, and a sense of home. Would he stay here and make a life with her in the castle, now the eternal winter had ended, or could she brave the outside world if he was by her side?

A waiter approached with a silver tray filled with crystal glasses of sparkling grape juice, and Astrid murmured her thanks and took a long drink, as she struggled to pull herself together. She was still trying to make sense of everything that had happened, from the breaking of the curse to the rush of joy when Emilja had forgiven her.

Casting a quick peek through the floor-to-ceiling windows, her heart brimmed over with happiness at the sight of the sunshine, and the vast expanse of green being revealed now the permanent snow had melted and the trees were shrugging off their thick winter blankets. She felt as reborn as the wild nature outside the castle, the future bursting with possibility, not just for her, but for everyone.

One thought still niggled at her though. "So Mother, I understand, kind of, that I broke the curse of eternal winter with my supposed sacrifice, but how did you remember to stop us forgetting?"

"It was your kindness that started to pierce my shroud of forgetting. Your concern for the guests at the ball, your remorse over what you did to Emilja, your generosity towards the villagers at the bottom of the mountain – yes, my steward told me about that – plus your worry over Finn and your kindness to Greta, even when you were plotting to entice him away from her. You saved us all with your compassion and your selflessness."

Moving closer, the Queen hugged her daughter, and Astrid almost fell apart at the unfamiliar, but very welcome, sensation. "I felt it this morning my darling, when you decided that Finn deserved to live the life he wanted, whether or not you were in it. Something shifted within you even though you didn't say anything, or know which way you would go. But I knew what you would choose, not consciously perhaps, but deep in my bones. I knew you would choose others before yourself. Your father would be so proud of you."

Tears trembled on the Queen's lashes, and Astrid was relieved when the castle steward appeared at her mother's side, took her elbow and gently guided her towards the door. "Thank you too, Finn," she called out, casting the words back over her shoulder like pearls.

Astrid's mind whirled, trying to weave together everything that had been revealed. Her mother loving her. Emilja forgiving her. The winter curse broken. Did this mean the time loop had ended? Glancing up at the clock, she almost cried with relief when she saw that it had finally ticked over to December 24. Time had been fixed. Christmas Day would come, the new year would bring her birthday, and the life-giving sun would restore them all. Crops would grow, animals would breed, and the seasons would recommence their dance. They would have food again, and the fear of scarcity and starvation would lift.

Smiling as Greta walked towards them, she snuggled further into Finn's arms. She was so grateful for his support, so happy to feel safe for the first time in her life. And she was thankful to Greta too, for having the courage to journey through forests, up mountains and across snowfields to find her friend, as well as the strength to challenge Astrid over her behaviour and her motives.

If this girl hadn't turned up on their doorstep, barefoot, blue-lipped and close to death, she would still be living in denial, battling the icy chill of winter, and thinking herself too undeserving to experience happiness. And she definitely wouldn't be standing here in Finn's arms, sharing words of love with this sweet boy.

"See, I told you that your life is just like a faery tale," Greta said with a grin, before kissing Astrid on both cheeks, hugging Finn tightly then heading outside, her delicate summer-pink dress swirling gracefully around her as she moved, her whole being glowing in the light of the reborn sun.

"Do you want to go outside too?" Finn asked softly, then smiled when Astrid immediately shook her head.

"I'm right where I want to be." She lifted a hand to caress his cheek, then gently stroked her thumb across his bottom lip. "I have all the warmth and sunshine I need right here, Prince Charming. Besides, this means it's finally Christmas Eve. I'm not sure if you noticed the sprig of mistletoe in my hair, but you'd better start kissing me."

Finn's eyes blazed. "I'll never stop wanting to kiss you."

Her lips curved up at the corners, her happiness palpable. "Blessed Solstice," she whispered, standing on tiptoes to gaze into his eyes. "I have a feeling it will be the best one I've ever had."

"Merry Christmas Astrid, my love."

Gently his lips met hers again, and she surrendered to the sensation.

Epilogue

"Your Majesty?"

Greta was on her way outside to feel the sun dancing on her skin, drawn to it like a moth to a flame. She was desperate to cast off the icy chill of the castle and sink into the bone-deep warmth that marked the end of the kingdom's eternal winter, but she paused in alarm when she saw the distress on the Queen's face. Was she *crying*?

As soon as the other woman realised she'd been spotted, a mask slipped quickly into place, and the monarch met her gaze with steely, hostile eyes. Or were they just sad? Overflowing with a pain she was trying so hard to shut off, and hide away?

"Are you all right?" Greta asked, then gulped. Would she be punished for daring to question her?

The Queen glared at her imperiously, face halfway between anger and scorn, then she let out a surprised laugh. "I'm fine Greta, thank you for asking, but how are you? It can't have been easy to come all this way just to have your beloved snatched away from you."

They both turned back to the centre of the ballroom, where Astrid still stood with Finn, his arms around her and her head resting on his shoulder, the two of them silhouetted in pale, golden light. They swayed together, to music only they could hear, oblivious to the fact that they were alone on the dance floor, since every guest was now celebrating outside in the sunshine.

Astrid lifted her head and gazed up at Finn, listening to something he said, and the tenderness as he stroked her cheek and smiled down at her made Greta burn with longing. To have someone look at her like that...

Swallowing over the lump in her throat, she focused back on the Queen. "It turns out he was never my beloved, nor I his, but he is my dearest friend, and I'm really happy that he's found someone so perfect for him."

"Not even the tiniest bit jealous?"

Greta's eyebrows shot up in disbelief, not sure she'd heard correctly. "Um, no, not jealous. My quest to find Finn was never about me being with him, or even taking him home, necessarily. I just needed to know that he was safe and happy. That he was where he wanted to be, not dead in a ditch, or trapped somewhere he couldn't return from."

"That's very noble of you," the Queen said, her eyes boring into Greta's, as though she was reading every secret written on her heart.

Was she?

Shifting uncomfortably, she stared down at her borrowed crystal-studded slippers in an effort to break their connection. "Well, when I set out from home I suppose I did think I would swoop in and rescue him. That I'd find him and free him, then we'd return home together to get married and live happily ever after, blah blah blah," she admitted.

"Yet by the time I finally got here and found him, I'd realised that I no longer wanted that life, and fortunately nor does Finn. I'm content to have spoken to him, and to have seen how happy he is with Astrid. That's enough for me – I don't have to actually be with him. But this world is a better place just knowing that he's somewhere in it, living his life, following his dreams. Wherever he chooses to be."

As she gazed out the windows, it was the Queen's turn to raise an eyebrow. "That's very mature of you."

"Not as mature as your daughter," Greta retorted, then paused, nervous about pressing the Queen further. But she'd be leaving in the morning, so what did she have to lose?

"Why are you so mean to Astrid?" she blurted, before she could talk herself out of it. "Your grand announcement to her just then made it sound like you love her, yet she thinks you hate her, and can't bear to be around her. Are you trying to drive her away?"

For a moment Greta thought the Queen was going to strike her, and she flinched, cursing herself for her impertinence. But eventually the older woman sighed, and ushered her to a table. They sat together, facing each other warily, and when the castle steward came over with a bottle of honey mead and two glasses on a silver tray, they allowed him to pour the drinks, then both hastily knocked them back and held out their glasses for a refill.

"Of course I love her," the Queen hissed, voice trembling with emotion. "And I regret how I've treated her, that I've hurt her, but it was for her own good that I was keeping my distance. I was trying to protect her."

Greta scoffed. "You haven't protected her, you've traumatised her. What possible reason could you have to do that, to push her so cruelly away, and belittle her in front of other people? She's scared of you, yet she wants so desperately for you to love her."

The Queen's eyes flashed with sudden anger, but a moment later her face crumpled and her shoulders sagged, the fury dissipating as quickly as it had come. "Eighteen years ago I did a terrible thing, an unforgiveable thing, and that's why I've kept myself aloof from my daughter, and not let her close. I've been terrified to let her know the real me, scared I would somehow infect her with my poison, or harm her even more. I thought she'd be better off brought up by strangers than by me. It devastates me that she despises me, but I couldn't risk her getting close."

Tears trickled down her cheeks, glittering like diamonds, or the hailstones of a violent inner storm.

Greta could feel the other woman's pain in her own body, sharp, icy and jagged. "There's nothing you could have done that's as bad as you're imagining," she assured the Queen. "What on earth did you do that you think you're not worthy of forgiveness, or your daughter's love?"

Draining her glass, the Queen looked Greta dead in the eyes. "I killed my husband." Suddenly she was the Snow Queen again, and Greta recoiled in fear, a chill running up her spine. *Did she really just say that?*

"You heard me. I killed my daughter's father."

Greta was stunned, and speechless.

Picking up the bottle of mead – which clearly displeased the castle steward, who dashed over, ready to be of service – the Queen refilled her glass, knocked back the golden liquid, then poured another, her hand unsteady as she lowered it to the table. "Is that bad enough?" she demanded.

"The King didn't die in a hiking accident, like everyone thinks, he died by my hand, and I'll never be able to forgive myself – or tell Astrid that it was me who robbed her of her father." Suddenly her eyes were imploring Greta, as though she was desperate to be understood. To be absolved.

"No." Greta couldn't believe that. She wouldn't.

"Yes. I'm the devastated wife of Edvard, who I killed with my bitterness and rage. But I didn't mean to, I swear."

"What happened?" Greta asked, horrified, and hardly daring to breathe, worried that it would distract the Queen from revealing the rest of her story.

"One night I went down to the kitchens and made us hot chocolate, then took it back up to the library. There was nothing we liked more than snuggling up in there by the fire and talking for hours." She smiled wistfully, and her face relaxed, the haunted look in her eyes momentarily dissolving as she thought of her beloved.

"When I walked back in though, there was a woman draped all over my husband, and they were kissing passionately." Her cheeks flushed with fury, but in an instant it was replaced with sadness and yearning, and Greta couldn't believe this broken woman was the same person who had been so arrogant and overbearing when they'd first met, or the regal royal who had welcomed guests to the Yule ball just a few hours ago with such confidence, and an attitude of quiet superiority.

The Queen's voice rose from its barely-there whisper, gathering pace and volume until it was as though a dam had burst and she could no longer stop herself. As though she was relieved to finally be unburdening herself of her dark secret. "I turned white-hot with rage, then went icy cold, and this... Energy? Power? Surge of ice? – rushed out of my hands, right at them, and obliterated both of them where they stood. I whirled around when someone came in behind me, almost hitting them too. And when I looked back, they were both gone."

The Queen's usually cold, stern eyes were wild, haunted, and Greta realised she was back in that long-ago moment, reliving the pain of her husband's betrayal, and of the punishment she'd unleashed in response. Placing a gentle hand on the distraught woman's shoulder, she smiled tentatively when she caught her gaze.

"But you didn't want to hurt your husband?"

"Of course not!" she burst out. "I'm not a monster! Why do you think I've cut myself off from the world? From my daughter? I was terrified that I'd hurt her too, or worse. Terrified she'd discover what I'd done and hate me as much as I deserved. And she did, but not for the right reason."

The Queen paused, trying to compose herself enough to continue. "But my husband? He's the love of my life, still. I've never even looked at anyone else, in the eighteen years since he... left me. I love him more than life itself, so sometimes it's hard to even look at Astrid, to be reminded every day of what I lost, and what I did to both of us. Taking her father away from her before she had a chance to meet him – before he got to meet her. He didn't even know I was pregnant. I was going to tell him that night, when I got back to the library. I was so excited, so full of hope."

She broke down in tears, and Greta stood up and reached out a hand, wanting to comfort her, to take some of her pain, but the steward already had an arm around her. It was the first time she'd seen him dare to touch the Queen, and as he stroked her hair and spoke soothing words, she collapsed into him. It was as though her frozen heart had shattered, and eighteen years of repressed guilt and anger, and fear and distress, were spilling out of her in loud, choking sobs that racked her body mercilessly. The mask of the stern, hyper-controlled monarch had disappeared altogether, and she was just a heartbroken woman grieving for the man she loved.

The moment stretched out, and Greta slumped back down in her seat, marvelling at the care in the steward's eyes, in the tender way he held the Queen, and the trust she obviously felt towards him. Had Astrid ever seen this side of her mother? Had anyone?

"You've loved him all this time," she said finally, wonderingly, and the other woman glanced up sharply, then tried to smile through her tears.

"Always," she murmured. "There will never be anyone else. I will love him until the day I die."

There was a golden shimmer around them, and a blast of warm air, and Greta peered anxiously through the haze. But it didn't look like anything had changed. Astrid and Finn still stood together in the middle of the ballroom, lost in each other, and everyone else was laughing and dancing and drinking outside on the grass.

"Did you feel that?"

The Queen nodded, as mystified as Greta, then she seemed to become aware that the steward was still supporting her. Embracing her. She straightened her shoulders, trying to appear regal once more, but a small smile hovered as she gazed at the man comforting her, and Greta was stunned to see the warmth between them.

"Your Majesty," he said softly, reverentially. "How can I help you?"

"Cal, I'm fine, I promise. I was just..." She hiccupped, and the steward leaned forward and gently wiped a tear from her cheek. Her face softened. "I was just telling Greta here about my beloved husband. How much I miss him still, every minute of every day."

He gaped at her, brow furrowed. "But I thought –"

Now it was the Queen's turn to stare. "What?" she demanded angrily. "What did you think?"

The steward paled, and staggered a little, as though he was drunk, the hand that had been on the monarch's shoulder suddenly clutching at the wall to stay upright. "You really loved him? You love him still?"

"Of course. I'll go to my grave loving him, and only him," she said, eyes downcast, so she didn't notice the ripple across the steward's face, the subtle rearranging of his features. Greta stared at him in wonder.

"I've always loved him, and I always will," the Queen continued, voice still muffled against his shoulder. "Why do you think I've never even looked at another man? That I've turned down every single potential suitor without meeting them? He will have my heart always."

The shimmering and blurring around the edges returned, and Greta felt dizzy. Was it her that was shimmering, or the castle steward? "What's happening?" she demanded, and the panic in her voice made the Queen look up at last.

When she followed Greta's gaze and looked at her steward, she shrieked, then covered her mouth in shock. He raised a quizzical eyebrow.

"*Edvard*?" the Queen asked, voice teetering on the edge of a precipice. Hysteria, or redemption?

He pushed aside the mead bottle and peered down into the silver tray, then raised a hand to his face in wonder. His chin had narrowed, and his brown eyes were now blue. His beard was gone, and his dark hair was now the same pale blonde as Astrid's. "Margrete?"

Bewildered, Greta looked from one to the other, then at the huge portrait above the dais, of the Queen and her husband on their wedding day. That man was standing before her now, a little older and more wrinkled, a little greyer, but reaching for his bride with the same adoration on his face – reaching until they were in each other's arms again, in an embrace that looked as though they would never let go of each other, no matter what.

"My love," the Queen was saying, as incredulous as Greta. Her smile was wide, and finally reached her eyes, the first time Greta had seen that occur. "What? How? Oh, I don't understand."

Her husband shook his head, but he was just as ecstatic as she was. "I don't either. All I remember is you coming to sit with me by the fire, you kissing me – and then the actual you walked in and…"

Margrete cringed. "And hurt you. I thought you were dead!" she cried. "I thought I'd *killed* you."

"Darling, you couldn't kill me, you wouldn't. How could you think that?"

The distress had returned to the Queen's face, and Greta's heart ached for her. "I didn't know what I'd done. And when I turned back around you were gone. There was no one there, not you or the woman, whoever she was."

Edvard frowned, pained by the reminder. "I don't know who it was. She looked *exactly* like you. Do you have an identical twin I don't know about?"

Shaking her head, the Queen cautiously met his eye. "I thought you were having an affair with her," she murmured.

"Oh darling, never. I thought she *was* you! She told me how excited she was about our child, how much she wanted it, and I was so deliriously happy. But then you came in with the hot chocolate, and I couldn't figure it out. It all happened so fast, like a bolt of lightning short-circuiting my brain, then everything went dark. I don't know how long it was until I finally regained consciousness," he said softly, sadly.

"As soon as I did, I went to find you, to check if you were okay, but Cook intercepted me. She glared at me as though she'd never seen me before, then asked if I'd come about the castle steward position. I didn't know what else to do, so I said yes. Fortunately, me knowing you so well meant that I passed her test with flying colours."

They both laughed, and Greta was struck by how well they fit together. Two halves of one whole. The yin and the yang. The piece of the puzzle that was bringing the Queen back to life, and the King back to himself, literally. But there was no escaping how tragic their story was. No wonder the Queen had kept her distance from her daughter, if she'd thought all this time that she'd killed her own husband, and denied their child a parent. What a terrible burden to live with, made even worse because it wasn't true.

Poor Astrid too, never knowing her father, or her mother either. Not the real her. Greta grimaced. Thank goodness she'd found the courage to press the Queen tonight, nervous though she'd been. What if she hadn't? Would mother and daughter have lived out their entire lives in such tension and disharmony? It would have affected Finn too, having a mother-in-law at such odds with his wife.

Stifling a giggle, Greta took a sip of mead. Perhaps she was getting a little ahead of herself, trying to marry them off already. She tuned back in to the happy couple.

"It took a few days for me to comprehend that I was in a different body, and nobody knew me, and I still can't get my head around that. Plus I had to remember not to let on how well I knew all the staff – or accidentally give them orders," the King said wryly, a twinkle in his eye.

The Queen grinned. "I would have liked to see that! I can just picture Cook's face if the lowly castle steward had told her to do something."

Edvard smiled too, but his eyes swam with tears. "It was the heartbreak of you not knowing it was me that was the hardest thing to cope with. It was like a knife in my chest each time you looked at me and didn't see me," he admitted, voice low and cracked with emotion.

"I so desperately wanted to hold you, to comfort you, to just talk to you, like we used to, sitting by the fire and chatting quietly about what we'd done that morning, or debating more serious things. Or reading in companionable silence, curled up on the couch together, or walking through the woods hand in hand – all the tiny, lovely, seemingly insignificant things we used to do. It wasn't the extravagant balls or the diplomatic missions or the ruling beside you that I missed, it was just being together, even if we weren't doing anything, that made life so wonderful."

Cupping her cheek, he leaned in and kissed her forehead, with a tenderness that gave Greta butterflies.

"I'm so sorry I didn't realise it was you, my love," the Queen said, and her face was hot with shame.

But her husband shook his head. "No my darling, you weren't to know. You can't take that on."

"You knew me though." Her voice was small, timid, and full of regret and apology. The proud, stern monarch Greta was familiar with had completely disappeared.

"Of course I did, but you looked like you. You *were* you," he said kindly. "You hadn't changed at all, you remained completely yourself, so it was easy for me. But how could you have possibly known that your loyal steward was actually your missing husband?"

Gently he stroked his wife's hair, and Greta's heart melted at the depth of his love for her. Would anyone ever look at her that way, with such devotion and admiration, so much strength and protectiveness?

"And you suffered more than enough in your own way," the King continued. "It was killing me to see you in pain all this time, yet not be able to tell you who I was, or that I was there for you. That I loved you." His voice broke.

"I tried to, so many times, but I was physically incapable of saying the words. Each time I started to explain, the words died in my throat, bitter ashes of all I wanted to share with you and Astrid. She must think me so silly, all those times I started speaking to her, trying to tell her who I was, when my voice would cut out halfway through a sentence." His gaze went to his daughter, still swaying in Finn's arms, oblivious to all that was unfolding, then returned to his wife, eyes filled with wonder.

"You must have thought me stupid too, my love. I used to be so eloquent, before this, but somehow the curse wouldn't let me utter a single word about who I was or what you meant to me."

The curse.

Greta stared at the Queen. She supposed the monarch's unleashing of her powers against her husband had triggered *this* curse, and maybe her revelation tonight that she had remained true to him all this time – eighteen long and lonely years – had broken it. But what about the other woman, the one who'd looked so like the Queen, and set the whole thing in motion?

"Who was she?" the Queen asked.

Edvard shrugged sadly. "I wish I knew. I swear to you, she looked exactly like you, enough to completely fool me. It wasn't just a passing resemblance, like your sister – I was absolutely convinced that it *was* you."

They both sighed in unison, and Greta tried to hide her amusement. They were like an old married couple, even though they'd only had a short time together before the curse was activated. Admittedly Edvard had spent a lot of time around his wife, watching her at least, but she wouldn't have been the same woman he'd married, transformed as she was by his supposed death into a grieving widow. And a stern, bitter, sometimes-harsh monarch, who'd kept their daughter at arm's length, or worse.

Greta desperately wanted to leave the table, to give them some privacy, but reminding them of her presence now would be too awkward. Best they stayed oblivious, wrapped up in each other and their eternal love.

Hunching down in her seat, she sipped the mead and tried to be as unobtrusive as possible. Yet with every word they uttered her heart broke a little more. She'd envied Astrid for her assumed cushy life, then pitied her when she learned of her ill treatment at the hands of her mother. Now she wanted to cry for all three of them. How tragic that their family had been so torn apart.

As though he'd heard Greta's thought, Edvard spoke again to his wife. "Each night as you cried yourself to sleep, I would sneak in to watch over you, tormented by your sadness but unable to do anything to help you. My heart hurt to watch you during your pregnancy, to see you suffering physically and emotionally, but not be able to reach you, or comfort you."

"But you were a comfort to me, in your other guise," the Queen said softly. "Not the comfort of a husband, true, yet you were always there for me as my steward, you were always kind to me, even when I was cruel to you. I must admit, I sometimes wondered why you stayed. It wasn't even that I meant any of my nasty words."

"Oh darling, you were just so sad. You didn't mean it. I never blamed you for that."

The Queen smiled. "You were so kind to me, I should have suspected. You brought me my favourite foods when I had cravings, and sometimes you seemed to anticipate what I needed before *I* even knew. I did occasionally wonder if you had a touch of the uncanny in your blood, some relative who was a witch."

He laughed. "Just my beloved wife. Although it pained me to hear people speak of you that way."

Margrete shrugged, then tried to muster a smile. "That was the least of my worries. 'Snow Queen', 'Winter Witch', 'Storm Crone' – I copped them all. But I have to thank you for your stroke of genius, the story that you'd died in a hiking accident. That I was the tragically young widow who needed time and space to grieve, rather than the woman who murdered her husband – or whose husband had despised her so much that he left her."

"I would never leave you!" he insisted, leaning forward to gently wipe a tear from his wife's cheek, his love for her blazing in his eyes like fire. "More than anything I wanted to be here, to help you cope in any way I could. But as time passed, I did have moments where I wasn't sure if I should stay, or if it would be better for both of us if I left, so you could move forward. I wondered if having me close was subconsciously stopping you from looking for a new husband. And yet, you never did. You had no interest in anyone else."

"Of course not!" the Queen said, voice urgent, almost outraged. "I married you, my love, and I've never wanted anyone else, even knowing that meant I would be alone forever. But I didn't want that for Astrid, and I'm glad she did have you, in some tiny way."

The King lifted the lock of hair that had fallen into Margrete's eyes and tucked it behind her ear, his hand lingering on her neck. Greta yearned for someone to touch her with such tenderness. To look at her the way Edvard was looking at his wife. The love in his eyes was making the Queen unfurl in response. She was blossoming, shedding the thorns she'd held around herself as protection all these years, daring to be vulnerable now her love had returned. She was a completely new person, her face open and carefree, and Greta was stunned by the transformation. Stripped of her pain and worry and grief, she was a beautiful woman, and her sparkling eyes and dazzling smile as she clung to her husband made her as radiant as any goddess.

She was thrilled for Astrid too. Not only did she have her father back, but her real mother had returned as well. From feeling so alone just that morning, her friend now had both her parents, and Finn's heart too.

Trying to bury the whisper of jealousy stirring within her, she focused back on the King. Edvard's soul was also shining, bright enough to light up the whole castle.

"I couldn't have left you anyway, even if it would have helped you in some way," he was telling his wife. "The only blessings I had in my new upside down world were being around you, however limited that was, and seeing our sweet daughter grow up. It was from afar for the most part, but occasionally I could be close to her, be kind to her. Although it was an exquisite pain too, to be able to watch her but not help her, not intervene. To not be able to tell her who I was, and how proud she made me. Oh Margrete, you should have seen her when she went down to the village at the bottom of the mountain. She was extraordinary."

They both turned to the dance floor and watched Astrid with Finn. The young couple had remained completely oblivious to the magic being done, or undone, before Greta's eyes, too wrapped up in each other, in their own love spell. It wasn't a spell cast on them by an external force though, it had been created by the respect and trust and courage they'd invoked together over recent weeks, the things they'd thought and shared and learned, and the goodness in both their hearts.

The Queen suddenly stared at Greta, and she gulped. She really should have let them have this conversation alone. But Margrete surprised her by smiling, and leaning over to refill her glass.

"Darling," she said to her husband. "Why don't you go and introduce yourself to Astrid?"

Standing abruptly, he kissed the top of his wife's head, bowed in Greta's direction, then hurried across the dance floor towards his daughter.

"Your Majesty," Greta said nervously, pulse racing and palms beginning to sweat. "I'm so sorry I…"

The Queen held up her hand. "You don't have anything to apologise for – I want to thank you. I'm so grateful to you Greta. No one has ever had the guts to challenge me, to ask me why I was so awful to my daughter, or force me to reveal what I did, and without that I would never have known that my beloved was still alive, and had always been with me. He would never have returned to me."

Her voice shook as the reality of her situation sank in. "You said you wanted to save Finn –"

"Astrid saved Finn," Greta said quietly.

"Perhaps. But you saved *me*." Tears welled in the Queen's eyes, and this time they were glittering diamonds. Precious gems born of love and joy, not the hailstones of her previous storm.

Greta forced a smile, trying to be gracious. Trying to keep the bitterness from her voice. But she'd never felt more alone. "And who will save me?"

A commotion at the door of the ballroom dragged their attention in that direction, then someone pushed past the guards and raced towards them.

"Greta! Oh thank god, I've found you!"

"The smallest act of kindness
is worth more than the grandest intention."
Oscar Wilde, Irish playwright and poet

Discover Greta's story in

The Sun Queen's Apprentice.

"No act of kindness,
no matter how small,
is ever wasted."
Aesop, Greek storyteller

Thank You!

Thank you so much for reading this book,
and sharing the wintry magic of Astrid,
Finn and Greta's stories.
As an indie author, I rely on word of mouth and
reader reviews to get the word out. If you enjoyed
The Snow Queen's Daughter, I would be so grateful if you
could take a moment to leave a review on any book site,
or tag me on facebook or instagram if you post about it.
Reviews can help improve sales and ranking, and are of
immense help to all indie writers. Even a single sentence
will make a difference, and might help a new reader
decide to give it a try.

If you'd like to stay in touch and receive free exclusive
content, be the first to hear about book news, events info
and giveaways, win prizes and more, you can sign up for
my very occasional newsletter at

www.sereneconneeley.com/subscribe.

(And don't worry, you can unsubscribe at any time...)

With love and gratitude,
Serene xx

With Love and Respect

I acknowledge the Gadigal People of the Eora Nation as the Traditional Custodians of the land on which I live, write and walk. I recognise their continuing connection to land, waters and culture, and their history of storytelling, and pay my respects to their Elders past, present and emerging.

And I acknowledge the Traditional Owners of Country throughout Australia. Like many nations, we have a brutal history of invasion and colonisation, and I am relieved and hope-full that our new government is starting to reflect the will of the people for change, and taking action towards recognition and reconciliation.

#voicetreatytruth
fromtheheart.com.au

With Thanks

I am so grateful, as always, to my sweet hubby and precious beloved, for his love, support, belief in me, and all the cups of tea while I write. Thank you for being my forever love.

Love and gratitude to my incredible writing bestie Selina Fenech, for support, encouragement, story feedback, making our enchanting joint project so magical, and being the sweetest person I know; to Kastie Pavlik, for late night/early morning rants and raves, valuable comments on Astrid and her motivation, and kindness and friendship across the oceans; and to Quinn Nichols, for editing the earliest version of *The Snow Queen's Daughter,* when it was a teensy 15,000 words, and needed US spelling.

Much love to Jo, Roslyn, Allana and the Sydney Ring of the Australian Fairy Tale Society (australianfairytalesociety.org), for faery-tale fun, friendship and inspiration. It's always a joy to drink tea, share stories, plan events, and discuss life, love, politics and faery tales with you. Remember when we were researching Hans Christian Andersen's story, and I kept asking *why* the Snow Queen would kidnap a boy? Here's my lengthy attempt at an answer.

And all the gratitude to Mum, Dad, Margie, Pete and my wonderful family, who have loved and supported me always, and to Voula, Kim, Elisabeth, Lucy, Jo Avalon and all my gorgeous friends, for bookish chats, tea and scones, fitness fun, and care, concern and commiseration.

With much love, Serene xx

"You cannot do a kindness too soon,
because you never know how
soon it will be too late."

Ralph Waldo Emerson,
American philosopher and poet

About the Author

Serene Conneeley is an Australian writer with a fascination for history, travel, ritual, and the myth and magic of ancient places and cultures. As well as her novels, non-fiction titles and oracle decks, she's written for magazines about news, travel, health, spirituality, entertainment and social and environmental issues, edited several kids mags and Australian Geographic publications, and contributed to books on witchcraft, history and personal transformation.

She is a member of the Australian Fairy Tale Society, and has studied magical and medicinal herbalism, bereavement counselling, reconnective healing, reiki and many other healing modalities, plus politics and journalism.

Serene loves reading books, drinking tea, working out, visiting the swans in her backyard park, and celebrating the energy of the moon and the magic of the earth. Her pagan heart blossomed as she climbed mountains, sat in stone circles, crawled into ancient burial mounds and stood in the shadow of the pyramids on her travels, and she's also, perhaps more importantly, learned the magic of finding true happiness and peace at home.

www.SereneConneeley.com

Other Books by Serene

The Into the Mists Trilogy

Into the Mists

Into the Dark

Into the Light

Into the Mists: A Journal

The Into the Mists Trilogy Hardcover Omnibus

"I'm absolutely blown away by this series. It is beautiful from start to finish – magical, realistic, gentle, harsh, sad, joyful... I've been on a total rollercoaster ride, and now feel totally bereft at the thought that these wonderful people will no longer be part of my life. These books are just beautiful."

Kylie Matthews, reviewer

The Into the Storm Trilogy

Into the Storm

Into the Fire

Into the Air

The Into the Storm Trilogy Hardcover Omnibus

"This series is a transformative must-read. Profound, thought provoking and empowering, it's so immersive that the magic emanates from the pages. I loved every second of it."

Kastie Pavlik, author of the Children of the Morning Star Trilogy

Practical Magic: An Oracle For Everyday Enchantment

Original Faery Tales

The Swan Maiden
The Snow Queen's Daughter
The Sun Queen's Apprentice

The Magic Series (with Lucy Cavendish)

The Book of Faery Magic

Mermaid Magic: Connecting With the Energy
of the Ocean and the Healing Power of Water

Witchy Magic

"*Mermaid Magic* is a wonderfully inspiring read. It really made me want to shed my twenty-first century shackles and dive into the ocean to embrace its wonderful healing powers. Thank you magical ladies for the journey!"

Sabina Collins, reviewer

The Sacred Series

Seven Sacred Sites: Magical Journeys That Will
Change Your Life

A Magical Journey: Your Diary of Inspiration,
Adventure and Transformation

Sacred Journey: A Meditation to Connect
You to the Magic of the Earth

"*Seven Sacred Sites* is by far the best travel book this year. Serene's style evokes the great travel writers like James A Michener, who weave cultural anthropology into an entertaining traveller's tale. It's a recipe for pure reading pleasure."

Joanne Lock, Spheres magazine